-2

Wabi-Sabi

Francesc Miralles

Translated by Julie Wark

ALMA BOOKS

ALMA BOOKS LTD
3 Castle Yard
Richmond
Surrey TW10 6TF
United Kingdom
www.almabooks.com

Wabi-Sabi first published in Catalan by Ara Llibres SCCL in 2014
This translation first published by Alma Books Ltd in 2016

The translation of this work was supported by a grant from the Institut Ramon Llull

llll institut ramon llull
Catalan Language and Culture

Printed in Great Britain by CPI Group (UK) Ltd, Croydon CR0 4YY

ISBN: 978-1-84688-398-9
EBOOK: 978-1-84688-407-8

It is better to travel full of hope than to arrive.

JAPANESE PROVERB

Prelude

We come from nothing and are headed for nothing. In between, we are something. This something is what we call life.

There was a time when I was obsessed with measuring this spark between the darkness that comes before us and what comes afterwards. I thought of existence as a sort of bag more or less filled with hours, days, months and years, and it made me anxious to think that every minute lived was one minute less in the countdown towards some place I didn't know. I wasn't in any hurry to get there either.

I hadn't yet understood that a few seconds of intense happiness leave a deeper mark in the spirit than a lifetime of monotonous waiting.

Until I was thirty-seven I lived in a prison cell of solitude I had built myself, brick by brick. Having closed the walls around me, I buried the key so no one could get in.

Then a stray cat came along, managed to dig up the key and, with his feline wiles, made me open up to the world. I've been sharing my life with him – Mishima is his name – ever since, together with an assortment of odd bods encountered along the way.

I live in a flat in the Barcelona neighbourhood of Gràcia. My elderly upstairs neighbour, Titus, writes inspirational books, and I sometimes help him out, when my teaching commitments at the university allow.

Mishima led me to him, and brought back Gabriela. I'm in love with her, though I know almost nothing of her past – or even of her present when she's not with me. Maybe that's why she doesn't want to live with me. So now I'm forced to be trendy: one couple, two flats.

Once I had a friend called Valdemar: an eccentric physicist who was exploring the dark side of the moon, but he vanished one day, leaving his telescope set up in Titus's kitchen. He also left us a manuscript detailing the results of his research and an unfillable vacuum – the kind left by people who mean something to us.

When Titus and I start missing him, we set up the telescope in Titus's kitchen again and point it at the moon, as if Valdemar had found out how to get there and would be sending us signals any moment.

He'll be back one day, or we'll go back to him because all of us are together in this great, always simmering cosmic cauldron in which no ingredient is wasted.

Over time I've learnt that solitude isn't the way to go about discovering yourself. You do that through other people. Once you've given up everything, it's relatively easy to climb a mountain and sit there doing nothing, letting the days slip by. It's more difficult – indeed it's the supreme art – to have a relationship with someone who's different from you. This is where your skills reveal your true measure as a human being.

I suppose I'm just a novice, because I'm always surprised by decisions made by the people around me. *Around me* can be taken in the broadest sense, as I was about to find out that first morning of June when I went downstairs and opened my letter box...

MANEKI-NEKO

The Beckoning Cat

We were nearing the end of the academic year, so I wasn't expecting to find anything in the letter box apart from flyers from the university, summoning me to staff meetings or announcing summer seminar programmes.

However, instead of academic junk mail, there was a postcard waiting for me. I held it up to the light so I could see it better: there was a picture of a porcelain cat with its left front paw raised.

When I turned it over, I expected to find the address of some new Chinese bazaar in the neighbourhood – the sort of place where you see these items – but, to my surprise it had a Japanese postmark. Besides my address, handwritten with a very fine nib, there was an extremely short message, just one hyphenated word:

WABI-SABI

Very puzzled, I stood there next to my letter box, flipping the card over time and time again, now looking at the photo, now at the mysterious word. I had no idea who could have sent me this from so far away, or why, but something told me that this innocent little kitty – well, that's if it really was innocent – was going to cause an upheaval. The last cat that came to my door, Mishima, had been a harbinger of havoc, so I wasn't going to take this lightly.

To begin with, the postcard cat changed my plans for that morning, so instead of going out I went back upstairs to the attic flat and rang at Titus's door.

It opened with a buzz – a sign that he was busy with one of the books he's commissioned to write. Indeed, as soon as I pushed the door open, I heard his fingers skittering over the keyboard against a background of jazz. Delicate ribbons of smoke snaked through the air. Yes, he was hard at work. Titus only burnt his incense sticks when he was writing.

Before emerging from the passageway into his living room-cum-study, I stopped for a moment before the reproduction of Caspar David Friedrich's *Wanderer above the Sea of Fog*. I'd seen it dozens of times, but that young romantic atop his high crag still impressed me.

"Are you going to stay out there?" The welcome was gruff.

I went into the living room, in the middle of which stood Titus's desk. He stopped typing and stared at me enquiringly.

"You're working..."

"Looks like it, wouldn't you say?" His tone was mocking. "I have exactly four days before the deadline for *A Cent a Laugh*, and I still have a quarter of the book to write, plus a prologue on laughter therapy.

"What a ridiculous title. What's it about?"

"It's a local version of an American book. An anthology of a thousand jokes selling for ten euros, or one cent for every dose of mirth."

"Very ingenious."

"It's not my idea, and I can't guarantee people will laugh at these jokes. I'm not at all amused by the ones I've found." He gestured towards the end of the table at a pile of books bristling with Post-It tabs.

"I'll let you get on with your work, then."

"Hang on a moment. What did you want to tell me?"

I weighed up the risk that Titus would order me to start looking for jokes for his book, but my curiosity about the postcard got the better of me, so I dropped it on the table. Then I sat on his couch waiting to hear what he had to say.

"That's interesting." He smiled. "Who sent you this?"

"I don't know. There's no sender there. Just that hyphenated word. Do you know what it means?"

"*Wabi-sabi…*"

Titus pronounced the word as if it were a magic spell. Just then, a softly whistling train started whirring round the tracks and through the tunnels of a miniature railway set he'd laid out on a table next to the wall.

"That almost scared me," I said. "How many buttons and switches have you got on your desk?"

"Only two. One to open the door and the other for the train set. As you know, it helps me concentrate. Anyway, I can't give you an answer right now, though I've seen this word before. Ask Gabriela. Didn't she once live in Japan?"

"She's in Paris and won't be back till next week. The porcelain cat might also be some kind of clue."

Titus traced its outline with his finger. "That's no mystery. It's a *maneki-neko*. There are millions of them in Japan."

"What's a *maneki-neko*?"

"Look it up in the third book on that shelf." Titus pointed at a bookcase on the far side of the room. "It's strange you don't remember, because you helped me write it."

"Valdemar wrote it in the end. Don't you remember?" I took *A Short Course in Everyday Magic* from the shelf.

He was right. In the chapter called "Feline Philosophy", there was a section about the *maneki-neko*.

MANEKI-NEKO: THE LUCKY CAT

Although this figure is very popular with Japanese shopkeepers, its origins must be sought in ninth-century China, where it was believed that a cat cleaning its ear with its paw was a sign that a visitor was coming. The animal was edgy before the arrival of a stranger and showed it with this gesture of washing its face and ears.

Some sources claim that the cat's story goes back to a real-life story in the Edo period (1603–1868). A cat named Tama was always on the porch of a temple built next to a large tree in the western area of Tokyo. One rainy day, a nobleman took refuge under the tree, and Tama kept trying to attract his attention by beckoning with a paw. Curious about the cat's behaviour, the man left his refuge and went to see why the cat was doing this. Just then, the tree was struck by a bolt of lightning, which also destroyed everything around it. Moved by the cat's solicitousness, the nobleman became a benefactor of the temple.

Another tale concerns a very poor woman called Imado. She could barely keep herself alive, so had to sell her cat. One night the cat appeared to her in a dream, telling her to make clay models in its likeness as a lucky charm. She obeyed the cat, and a passerby saw the figure and wanted to buy it. From then on, she made so many cats, which she sold to so many people, that she became rich.

"Most enlightening." I was mildly sarcastic. "But that doesn't tell me anything. Why would someone send me a lucky cat? I don't know anyone in Japan."

"It might be a sign that a stranger is arriving. Or maybe you need good luck for some adventure you're going to embark on soon."

These two possibilities sounded like prophecies by a sinister oracle. I knew from experience that the coming of a stranger always left a string of bothersome complications in its wake. As for adventures that require good luck, I'd call them calamities.

I still had to discover what "*WABI-SABI*" meant. Something told me I'd soon find out.

Endangered Animals

We'd finished classes in the Faculty of Philology, and my time was now taken up by curriculum planning meetings, invigilation and a few hours of tutoring for which hardly anyone turned up.

That Tuesday morning, I was amusing myself by watching how the summer light slid through the big window to light up a landscape of cracks and dust on my old office table. Suddenly I caught myself sighing.

Since I'd got my PhD in German Studies and started to work as a lecturer, everything had changed within the walls of that faculty building. The BA in German Philology which I had studied was no longer being offered, and the small pile of exam papers of the last group doing this course was now waiting for me in my office.

There were barely a dozen students in my class, so they were almost like family. After that, the course was "discontinued" – which is to say it was to become extinct just like other archaic, unnecessary wild species, and I was going to be subsumed into the English Department.

I, too, was an endangered species.

My literature classes were cut down to one, for PhD candidates. For the rest, I taught Goethe's language to students who found my subject too demanding. German is like a lover who respects you only if she has your exclusive attention. If it's taken as a minor subject by an English student, it can be hell. The long list of nouns with irregular plural forms and the declensions are enough to put anyone off, especially if they are taking only one or two classes a week.

Since the extinction of my degree course, therefore, I'd become a teacher of a language that brought more pain than joy to my students.

The only good thing about not having regular Literature students, I told myself, was that I didn't have to mark those exams – an almost impossible task in the Google era. Nowadays, correcting an essay on any author or work means major research trying to find out the sources of the students' plagiarism in that copy-and-paste mishmash they try to pass off as their own work.

When invigilating an exam in the classroom, I need a thousand eyes to make sure students aren't using their smartphones as an endlessly resourceful cheat sheet.

I was musing about all this when my office door flew open and I saw a mop of curly blond hair. The girl asked if she could come in. Snapping out of my forty-five-year-old lecturer's bout of nostalgia, I looked at her and noticed she had a triangular, cat-like face.

She was old enough to be a PhD student, but I'd never seen her before.

"Who are you looking for?"

"I don't know."

She came over to me and put a CD on the table. The cover sheet showed a circle drawn in a single brush stroke. It seemed to have been done by a master of Japanese calligraphy.

"I'd like to know the meaning of the words in this CD," she began in a low, melodious voice. "Could you listen, please – just for a minute?"

She took a Discman from her bag – an obsolete item in digital times. Another extinct animal. She loaded the CD and offered me the headphones, which were emitting a male voice speaking a strange language. I played my part of the lecturer in German with no time to waste.

"You should go to the School of Languages," I suggested. "We don't teach Japanese in this faculty."

"It's not Japanese," she corrected. "It's a dead language, and I want to understand it. Or at least know what language it is..."

Taken aback by this, I started listening. With guitar chords in the background, a young man was singing a strangely melancholy air. I couldn't make out a single word. It didn't seem to be any Semitic language, or Germanic language either.

The blonde girl waited impatiently for my verdict.

"I'm sorry to disappoint you." I handed back her Discman. "I haven't got a clue..."

She interrupted, "At first I thought it might be Elvish, but a friend of mine who's writing a thesis on Tolkien says that Elvish is completely different."

The cat-girl's phone started ringing, which gave me the perfect excuse to put an end to this bizarre conversation. I stood up, ready to usher her out, but she cut off the call and said, "I suspect it's Atlantean."

I was astounded. I'd been working in the faculty for seventeen years and no one had ever come to me with anything as weird as this. My penchant for oddities prevailed over prudence, so I asked, "What makes you think it's Atlantean?"

As soon as the question was out of my mouth, I realized how laughable, how preposterous it was for a university teacher to be asking such a thing. Atlantis only existed in a couple of hazy mentions by Plato. I'd never heard anything about any Atlantean language.

She returned the CD to its case and her phone rang again. She looked crossly at the screen and finally answered, as if in the privacy of her own home and not in a university office.

"Look, I told you, I never want to see or hear from you again. Didn't I say it clearly enough before?"

I deduced from the girl's exasperated expression that the person on the other end wasn't giving up easily. She answered harshly, backing towards the door. She waved goodbye from the corridor and closed the door behind her.

Disconcerted, I remained standing by the window for a few moments. A gigantic squalling gull flew by, its wings spread wide.

When I glanced back at my table, I was startled to see the CD of songs in an unidentified language still lying next to my pile of uncorrected exam papers. I rushed to the door, but there was no sign of the curly-haired girl.

Not even a treatise on the language of Atlantis could have been emptier than the corridor was just then.

Do You Speak Atlantean?

When I got home that afternoon, I had no idea that this meeting in my office was just a prelude to what awaited me in a day that was gearing up for disintegration on every front.

The cat had knocked over a vase that once belonged to Gabriela's grandmother. It was the only item of any sentimental value she'd left at my place, and she would be upset about this when she returned from Paris. I looked at the clock. Twelve minutes past six. She might still be working at the Contemporary Art Fair. I sent her a WhatsApp message.

Bad news, my love.
Mish broke yr g/m's vase.
Porcelain finer than I thought. Shattered. Sorry, can't be fixed.
Love you.
SAM

After sending my commiserations, I went looking for the cat. He was nowhere to be seen. He would have known he was in big trouble.

While waiting for Gabriela's answer – the two grey ticks showed that my message had gone through – I sat down on the couch with my laptop on my knees and briefcase beside me.

When I was looking for the card of another teacher I wanted to email, I found the CD complete with its Japanese circle. I'd brought it home in case one of my colleagues decided to throw it away and then that crazy girl wanted it back. Since I'm an inquisitive type, I couldn't resist putting it in the disc drive and playing it again.

The singer's voice rose and fell in a melody full of high and low notes, like the roller-coaster of life. I listened carefully once again, trying to make out words, but not a single one sounded familiar. Yet the intensity and passion of the singer made me think I knew exactly what he was saying.

Now caught up in the cat-girl's fascination with the CD, I inspected the cover sheet and, on the back of it, discovered a signature in tiny writing: Daniel Lumbreras.

This seemed an appropriate name for the only Atlantean speaker in the world, I thought, smiling to myself as I typed his name on Google and then Facebook. Although it's not a very common name, I found several people called precisely that, but the longish troubadour's haircut in a blurry photo of a young man from Barcelona made me think this was the one I was looking for.

So far so good. I sent him a private message on Facebook.

Samuel de Juan

Hi Daniel,

I might be writing to the wrong person, but I have here a self-recorded CD with a circle on the cover sheet and am wondering if it's yours. The girl who left it in my office thinks you sing in Atlantean. In that case, may I ask where you learnt it?

Thanks in advance for your attention and apologies for my intrusion.

After hitting the Enter key, sending off the message to someone who might not know anything about this matter, I told myself I hadn't changed much since the days when I used to enjoy reading a dictionary of untranslatable terms.

That was the moment when Mishima chose to reappear, his tail held high like an antenna trying to detect the mood in the living room after his mischief. He looked at me enquiringly and let out a faint miaow.

"All right, come on, up you come… I've swept up the mess you made and told Gabriela."

Mishima jumped onto the couch and rubbed his head against my ribs. Then my mobile beeped.

"That's her," I told him. "Let's see how she's taken it."

Samuel,

Don't worry re vase. Nothing lasts for ever.

Will you be home at 10?

We need to speak.

GAB xxx

Wave to Luck and Luck Will Wave Back to You

Filling in time till ten o'clock, I started reading a book Titus had given me about the *maneki-neko*, the lucky cat that had so mysteriously come to me in the form of a postcard from Japan.

Wabi-sabi, I said.

Having been distracted by the man who sang in Atlantean, I'd forgotten to find out what it meant. And now my laptop was shut down.

The book Titus gave me was by a German writer called Christopher A. Weidner. Since Titus used different names for the self-help volumes he wrote, I wondered at first whether this was a pseudonym, but the back flap offered a biography that was long enough to make me think that this was the author's real name.

The book consisted of a collection of stories about cats that brought good luck. The basic idea was: "Wave to luck and luck will wave back to you".

Wanting to find out how you go about waving to luck, I went to the last section of the book, in which Weidner tells you that to make a wish come true you have to meet six requirements:

1. The wish has to be really small.
2. It must be achievable right now or tomorrow at the latest.
3. It has to mark the beginning of something new and it must be something you're not going to leave half finished.
4. It must be something you can do independently of external factors like time or help from others.
5. It has to be something that can be formulated clearly.
6. It must suggest that change is possible.

While I was trying to think of a wish, I went to warm up some dinner. Mishima followed me into the kitchen, where I tipped a tin of ravioli in tomato sauce onto a plate and put it in the microwave.

As the plate revolved with this slop that was supposed to be my sustenance, I remembered a scene from *Seinfeld*. The star of the series goes with his friend to the launderette and, contemplating his clean socks and other items spinning round and round in the dryer, he says, "This is the dullest moment I've ever experienced."

I couldn't say the same, because Gabriela's message had made me uneasy. I wasn't worried about her wanting to talk at ten at night, because we chatted every night when she was travelling. What seemed ominous was the fact that she hadn't got upset about the broken vase – which, she believed, contained her grandmother's spirit.

Given her impetuous nature, a storm-by-phone was more than probable, but she'd only said, "Don't worry re vase." Was she indifferent about the mishap because something major had happened to her?

The phone rang. I'd soon find out.

I ran to answer it. Her quavering voice confirmed that something wasn't right. After a few botched attempts to form a sentence, she eventually asked, "What were you doing?"

"Reading a book about the *maneki-neko*," I told her, trying not to show my concern. "It gives you six rules for summoning up good luck and making a wish come true."

"And have you made your wish?"

"No. In fact I've just realized that my only wish was to talk to you, and now I'm doing that. Right now I don't need anything else."

There was silence her end. It was a little too long.

"Gabriela? Can you hear me?"

"I can hear you. I was just thinking…"

"What were you thinking?"

I could hear her breathing fast and loud at the other end of the line. I didn't understand what was going on and, while Gabriela was deciding about telling me what was bothering her, I blurted out, "Ah, I almost forgot! Before I started checking out the lucky cat – because I got a postcard from Japan but I don't know who it's from – I did something very strange. I wrote to a man I don't know. It seems that he sings in Atlantean. He must be the only one in the world. Isn't that…"

"Samuel," she interrupted. "I think we need to take a break."

This appeared to be an immediately self-fulfilling prophecy, because her words were followed by a long, heavy silence. Now I was the one who couldn't speak. Cold sweat ran down the back of my neck. The phone was my life raft. I clung to it, waiting for her to finish.

"No, don't imagine I'm with any other man. I'm not in love with anyone else. I know that's how it usually works, but it's not the case this time. I'm alone."

"Me too," I said, somewhat relieved. "We're two solitary spirits who found each other in the middle of the storm. Isn't that what we always say? That's why we keep our own flats."

"And it's been great, Samuel."

Her voice broke. I could hear her sobbing, even though she'd turned away from the phone. While I waited for her to come back, shock waves from the bomb of those words "it's been" laid waste to my head.

With all the courage I could muster, I tried to smooth over the situation by acting cool, even though I was falling apart by the second.

"Don't worry about me, Gabriela. We'll talk about it when you get back to Barcelona. Go and get some sleep now."

A third pause before the last stab. "I'm not coming back, Samuel."

Luminous Music That Makes You Feel Better Inside

Dear Friend,

I'm very flattered that a university teacher like yourself (yes, I checked you out and found your email address in the faculty directory – and prefer this to Facebook) should have listened to my CD and found it interesting.

I know the quality of the sound isn't very good. I decided to record the songs because I was starting to forget them. I've composed too many and there's not enough room for all of them in my head. Once I started recording them, I realized I could make a demo CD.

Despite the sound problem, I think the quality of the songs themselves hasn't been lost. Then again, the arrangement is always the same: always one voice and a guitar. As it has to be. From start to finish. The uniformity could make for monotonous listening.

As for the language, there is no language. It's voice as just another instrument. Pure improvisation. The melody's the same, but the sounds of the voice change. Those sounds are never repeated. This lets me create in a strict present and express the emotions I'm feeling that precise moment. It's strange, but I think the listener somehow picks up this immediacy.

My experience is that when I sing like this I'm able to express feelings I can't convey in words. I've always admired luminosity and (spiritual) power in my musical gurus. I like luminous music that makes you feel better inside, opens up a space of well-being, gives you strength and courage, and holds out hope.

If I manage to convey these values some day, I'll feel fulfilled.

I like to say that I can't be understood in any country, but everyone can understand me. There's something universal about that.

Moreover, the ego kind of dissolves. I think that language is essential to the construction of our identity. It helps us to think about ourselves.

When I'm singing I really don't feel as if it's me singing. I experience it as a void. There's no one there. Or maybe it's the opposite. I am more me than ever. Creating my own language, able to change from one moment to the next, like reality itself.

I'm a big fan of Nietzsche, Wittgenstein and Foucault, and their studies on language. How language determines your way of seeing and understanding the world.

But all this is just words. I'm complicating matters. The main thing is the music. And the fact that this urge I have to sing is natural and spontaneous. I believe it comes from an innocent, ingenuous spirit.

In fact, when I was a little kid and my brother and I were still sharing one room in bunk beds, I used to sing like this. He dropped off to sleep immediately and, up in my top bunk, I started to sing in the dark. I haven't got a clue what I was singing. I was just a little boy and didn't have CDs or favourite songs. I simply sang.

Anyway, as I've heard people say several times, the innocence of a child is unexceptional. The innocence of an adult is the result of hard work. I don't know whether I've kept it, or recovered it, or maybe I believe I have it when in fact I don't.

Well, as you can see, I love talking about these things. I get carried away. And, after all that, I haven't said much about music.

With warmest regards and hoping to hear from you soon!

Daniel Lumbreras

Sentimental Archaeology

It was four in the morning and I still hadn't reacted. Lying in my now cold bath, I let my thoughts travel back and forth between Gabriela's phone call and the long, profound email I had received.

All too often, things don't turn out as we expect. I thought there'd be a fuss about the broken vase, but no, there was no fuss. What had been broken, at least for the time being, was our relationship. I imagined that my question to the man who sang in Atlantean would be met with silence or a couple of brief lines: instead, I'd received a letter I would read and reread several times in the coming days.

The world is unpredictable, but wise people maintain that everything happens when it has to happen. That's the most worrying thing of all. I didn't understand why, after eight years together, Gabriela should have sunk our personal Atlantis.

Trying to ignore that fact that I was freezing in the cold water, I went back over our relationship, doing my best to understand how we'd got to that point. The point of her not coming home after a business trip that was supposed to last two weeks at the most.

Our beginnings had been strange and moving. I'd first met Gabriela when she was a little girl, and then we found each other again after we'd both turned thirty-five. After some months of dithering, we started going out together. Two and a half decades of not knowing anything about the other person gives you plenty to talk about.

After a period of mad lovemaking, the phase of sentimental archaeology begins. Each one feels obliged to look back over old relationships and explain why they failed. This can be boring, especially in the early days, when you just want to go and make love again. But it's good conversation fodder when you're walking in the park, dining out or lazing in bed after a night of passion.

There's something quite titillating in discovering what led your partner to other bedmates who are so different from you. It's also a good thing to find out what went wrong in previous relationships so you can avoid making the same mistakes. You want the love you're building now to last for ever.

In this early phase, I didn't have much to say for myself, because my loves had been more platonic than real. By the time I was thirty they weren't even platonic. I'd turned the whole world into a hostile place and withdrawn into my shell like a snail.

Gabriela had told me about three of her relationships that she thought were important. I imagined the rest were just messing-around. She didn't offer too many details, because she was set on wiping out the past as if, instead of clay, the stuff that made us what we are now is some base material that needs to be buried very deep.

It was especially difficult for her to talk about the years she'd spent in Japan, where she'd worked as an English teacher. She lived in Osaka and, when she wasn't with her students, she stayed in her rented room and read anthologies of short stories in English.

Something big must have happened to her there and led to her sudden decision to come back. She never wanted to tell me what it was. No way. She wouldn't talk about it.

To go back to sentimental archaeology, when this phase of establishing all the old stories comes to an end, the real challenge begins. The couple can no longer call on past miseries. Now there's only the present, which unfolds, generally without much fanfare, one day after another.

Instead of turning her on by telling her how you once hid between two cars and did it with a girl from your class, you talk about your day at work. In the beginning it's fun, because she doesn't know the actors in the little show performed, day in day out, in the theatre of work. But when one has sat through the same story a hundred or a thousand times, it starts to get wearing.

The problems are always the same, and the advice you can give your partner is always the same.

This is the point when the fascination that fuels the fire of love starts to die.

The Angel's Reasons

At five in the morning, when I was on the verge of catching pneumonia, I swapped the bathtub for the couch and a light blanket. Trying to find some kind of anchor to hold me to past happiness, I watched *Wings of Desire* for the umpteenth time.

It's strange to see how the passing of time affects modern classics like this film. In our era of smartphones and social networks, the pace of this black-and-white film is intolerably slow. We no longer know how to stay still in front of a screen where nothing is happening. Or almost nothing.

I was almost catatonic with shock, numbed by the cold bath water and sleeplessness. Maybe that's why I felt better listening again to the angel's reasons for giving up eternity.

It's great to live by the spirit, to witness day by day, for eternity, only what's spiritual in people's minds. But sometimes I'm fed up with my spiritual existence.

Instead of forever hovering above I'd like to feel a weight grow in me to end the infinity and to tie me to earth.

As my eyes were closing, I thought I'd felt something like that when I came down from my own sky of German authors and composers of classical music to love Gabriela.

The man who'd taken refuge from reality and left the world on the wings of art and culture had come down to earth again to experience the simple pleasures.

This was my last thought before I fell asleep.

The Golden Pavilion

I woke up before nine, wallowing in feelings even more wretched than those of the early hours of the morning.

In the confusion of the night, my drama had seemed to be part of a nightmare or alcoholic haze, although I hadn't drunk a drop. I'd felt authorized to project myself onto the angel in the film while humanity slept until the breaking of a new dawn.

In the cold hard light of day, however, I had no choice but to accept what I'd become: a man who was now unwillingly alone.

I decided to go to the faculty, although I had no exams or lessons. As I was shaving, I looked at all the grey hairs which had won the battle over the black ones. The bags under my eyes were more pronounced too, no doubt because of the tears I'd shed in the night.

Maybe you should phone her and ask how she is. I splashed some refreshing aftershave on my face. *They say the one who leaves suffers more than the one who's left.*

In keeping with my state of mind, I dressed in black. An exhausted, shambling beast, I dragged myself to the door and was about to go out when I saw a new postcard lying on the floor by my feet. The postman must have left it there early in the morning, perhaps on his way to deliver a recorded parcel to Titus.

It showed an elegant Asian temple surrounded by hills and water. It wasn't difficult to guess that the sender was the same person who'd sent me the cat which had brought me such ill fortune.

The writing on the stamp and postmark was in Japanese, but a few words in one corner revealed that the photo of this temple, the Golden Pavilion, had been taken in Kyoto. As with the first postcard, my name and address was written in ink, in beautiful handwriting.

It was disconcerting not to have a clue as to who was sending me these things, especially as I'd never been to Japan. The most disquieting thing was the space reserved for the message.

It was completely empty.

Umami

Too tired and confused to do anything useful, I then decided that my best option would be to change my routine that Tuesday, so I went upstairs to see Titus, looking for a little human warmth.

Just like every other day of the week, including Saturday and Sunday, he was sitting at his table surrounded by books and tapping away at his computer keyboard. Titus's body seemed to be shrinking a little more every day, but he never tired of working. His clean-shaven head made me think of Zen monks in temples like the Golden Pavilion.

Since I was still hurting too much from the blow I'd received, I started with the temple.

"I just got another postcard."

I put it down on the table, trying to make him look up from his computer. After a quick glance, he took off his glasses, cleaned them and examined both sides of the postcard.

"Looks like you have a faithful friend in Kyoto. The first one was from there too."

"Faithful friend? I don't know anyone in Kyoto – or anywhere else in Japan, for that matter. It must be a mistake."

"No one makes the same mistake twice. Anyway, your name and address are written here. This is no mistake."

I took a stool over to sit beside him, like a little boy wanting his father's advice and protection. I needed both. I was wounded, lost, a dog abandoned by the roadside.

Titus must have noticed something, because he put his hand on my shoulder and said, "I'm going to make a pot of *kabusecha*, and then we can have a good talk."

I stayed where I was, staring at Titus's trains. Crouched under the table where they were rattling around their tracks, Mishima – who'd followed me upstairs – watched with expectant eyes.

Titus returned with a cast-iron teapot and two irregularly shaped cups. "They're Japanese, like your friend." He winked at me. "We'll drink to his health. This is *kabusecha*, which is halfway between *sencha* and *gyokuro*. It's all a question of *umami*."

"I can't make head or tail of what you just said, Titus."

He sat down at his table, swivelling his chair round to face me, and filled the two small cups with the greenish liquid. The room now had a faint smell of fresh herbs.

"I recently started getting interested in tea", he explained. "My body's giving out, so I'm taking all the antioxidants I can to put off the evil hour."

I remembered the heart attack he'd had some years earlier and how I'd been obliged to take over his work as a writer. I hadn't shown the slightest talent.

"The three varieties I just mentioned represent three ways of growing the same plant." He was proud to show off his knowledge about his latest passion. "*Sencha* is the natural kind of green tea. It grows all by itself in the sun, from planting to harvest. At the other end of the spectrum is *gyokuro*, which is like the champagne of the green teas. Its final growth period is carefully shaded. Between these two varieties is what we're drinking now. Have a sip..."

I lifted the cup to my lips and tried the tea. It was mild and a little astringent.

"The *kabusecha* has just a touch of *umami* because it's slightly exposed to sunlight while the leaf's growing."

"What is *umami*?"

"It's the tea's special slightly bitter flavour." Titus's sunken eyes roamed over my face. "And, now that I think about it, there's a strong symbolic link between *umami* and human affairs."

He lifted his cup to inhale the fragrance of the *kabuse-cha* before taking a sip. I waited for him to continue.

"The less light the plant receives as it grows, the more *umami* it will have. The same thing happens with human emotions. If you don't air your worries, they ferment inside you and end up making you bitter."

"Have you read something like this in my face?"

"Yes. Out with it, Samuel. What's the matter?"

The Universe Moves

Titus kept his trains running round and round their tracks as I gave him a blow-by-blow account of the phone call the previous night. Every time they went over Mishima's head, he thumped the parquet floor with his tail. When I finished talking, Titus was still concentrating deeply on their circular progress. Then he slowly turned towards me and pronounced: "There's nothing you can do right now except for accepting the *wabi-sabi* of all things, including love."

"That word was written on the first postcard..." I was thinking aloud. "So, you've worked out what *wabi-sabi* means then?"

"I certainly have! So much so that Gottfried Kerstin has decided to write a whole *wabi-sabi* guide. I have a publisher who's interested, and I wrote the prologue today."

I was immediately on guard. I hadn't forgotten the time when Titus was ill and had roped me into writing one of his books.

"Read this and you'll see what I'm talking about."

He clicked on a document he had on his desktop. Indeed, Gottfried Kerstin was presenting a concept that is deeply rooted in Japanese culture.

The expression *wabi-sabi* opens into a whole aesthetic concept and at once a philosophy of life.

Wabi-sabi refers to the beauty of what is imperfect, temporary and incomplete. This idea, like so many other aspects of Japanese culture, is inspired by observation of nature. Nothing in nature is perfect – or at least not in the Euclidean-geometrical sense in which we conceive of perfection in the West, because it is full of asymmetries. Nothing is permanent in nature, for every living thing is born and dies and is undergoing constant change; nothing in nature is finished or complete because the idea of completion is just an abstraction created by the human mind.

The *wabi-sabi* philosophy appeared in response to sixteenth-century Chinese perfectionism, and is present in the tea ceremony, in *ikebana*, the Japanese art of flower arrangement, haikus and Noh theatre.

"Nothing is permanent," I repeated. "Is that what you meant when you were talking about love?"

"If we think of love as just another human art then, according to the Japanese, it would have to be in accordance with *wabi-sabi* principles. It's imperfect because every couple is the sum and friction of two imperfections. Love is unfinished because, for better or worse, relationships never stop evolving. And, yes, it is temporary or impermanent. You have to make the most of it while it lasts."

"Then… you don't think that love can be eternal, like it is in stories or romantic films made in Hollywood."

Titus stopped his trains, as if he had very clear ideas on the matter. Hunched in his chair and looking jadedly up at me, he declared, "No, it can never be that. Even the relationship of two people who get on marvellously well finishes one day, because one dies before the other." He sat there quietly for a moment, pondering his words. "Unless they do something stupid together, of course."

"You might be right," I sighed, "but that's no comfort when you've just been kicked in the teeth."

"Now you're feeling hurt, but that will also change."

I didn't know what to say. While talking to Titus, I was wondering how long it was since he'd been in love. He'd been alone ever since I'd known him. I only knew that he'd had a wife once, but he had left her because – according to him – she made him dizzy with her chatter, when all he wanted was peace and quiet.

"But Gabriela didn't say it's over either." I held my ground. "She only said she needed a break for a while. She's staying with some woman – a friend of hers. Maybe she'll come back after that."

"Or she might never come back. Don't get your hopes up, or you'll be running the risk of waiting for a bus on a cancelled route."

"I was hoping you'd cheer me up, Titus," I protested, "but you're just making it look worse and worse. Why can't we have a second chance? I wouldn't say it's finished for ever."

"The universe moves."

These disconcerting words put an end to the conversation. The minutes were ticking by, and Titus probably wanted to get back to his manuscript.

I thanked him for the tea and his efforts to help me, though I felt even gloomier than I had before coming up to see him.

I was about to leave, when he looked up and said, "If I were you, I'd go and visit that friend of yours in the holidays. It would do you good to get away from your everyday world."

"Which friend?"

"The one who's sending you postcards from Kyoto. Nothing ever happens without a reason. You know what I think about that. If those messages are coming to you right now, it means that you have to do your bit and discover something. Well, I'd go there if I were you."

Wabi-Sabi Love

I spent the rest of that Tuesday in bed, waiting for a call which never came. I'd written a couple of messages to Gabriela, but her answers were very curt. She'd shut herself away, and Heaven only knew when she was going to say something.

With my laptop on my knees, I tried to distract myself by delving into Titus's latest subject – the beauty of imperfection. Browsing on Google, I found a book, *Wabi-Sabi Love*, which had been published in 2012. Ironically, it was about the art of preserving love. Then I found a song with the same title, released two years earlier.

I listened to it on Spotify. A husky voice sang over distorted guitar chords:

Where is magic gone?
Clouds wrap your bright soul
Embrace me,
I'm a child now
Begging for a smile.

As often happens in these cases, the song seemed to be about my twisted story with Gabriela. Maybe it was true that, at some point in the eight years that we'd been together, the magic had gone without my noticing, and she had felt stifled by routine.

Or it might simply have been a problem of different expectations.

Although we never actually lived together, I liked the rituals we'd established. A couple of times a week I went to meet her after work – she'd left the record shop and was now working in an art gallery – or she came to get me. We'd go to see a film, always in the original version with subtitles, after which we'd have dinner, then go to her place or mine and make love. That was it, week after week. We rarely went out at weekends. She said it depressed her to be part of a herd, and she preferred to stay at home reading.

Stop complaining low,
Life is pure imperfection.
Things are bumpy and rough
That's what's so funny about it.

Once again I recognized in the words of 'Wabi-Sabi Love' something that Gabriela had always chided me for. She said I grumbled like an old man when the world didn't work the way I wanted, and that I couldn't go with the flow of life as it really was.

Every obstacle was proof for me that human beings have been thrown into a world with no cosmic justice. Things happen for no reason – and here I had a major disagreement with Titus – so there's no point in looking for the whys and wherefores. We are shipwrecked in the sea of chance.

Gabriela didn't like my way of seeing things. She preferred to believe that she was guided by destiny. It was destiny that now told her to break with me. Perhaps she thought I had nothing more to give her. I'd become predictable. Maybe, after a pause, she'd look for someone a little wilder. An artist perhaps – one of those promoted by her gallery?

She'd certainly have more things to talk about with him than with a demoted German lecturer living alone with a cat.

Getting comfortable on my feet, Mishima let out a miaow as if he could hear my inner lament. The song had finished, and so had my first – and perhaps last – love story.

Wabi-Sabi love,
Circles never close.
Let's crash
Our unwise dreams
Against the world.

How to Fight Loneliness

Still sunk in my lethargy, I selected on Spotify an album by Wilco – one of the few bands I enjoy (probably because it reminds me of the Beatles) when I'm not listening to classical music.

I've never understood why they called their album *Summerteeth*, but it's got some of the songs I like most – especially 'How to Fight Loneliness', which was just what I needed right then, even though the advice wasn't much use for someone like me.

I'm more the sort of old-fashioned man who weeps when he listens to Bach than the rocker guy who tries to blot out his heartache with drugs.

Given my pathetic situation, a therapist would say I should socialize if I want to move on. Staying at home with Mishima would only mean getting more and more obsessed with my *wabi-sabi* love, with a relationship which, like a fallen leaf, would never come back to life.

It's not easy, though, to make a list of your friends when you've got through your life without hanging out with anyone except your girlfriend and your social life is confined to a cat and an old writer who's always busy.

My list of friends would make anyone weep.

I suddenly started missing Valdemar, the eccentric physicist who studied the dark side of the moon. He wasn't easy, but I often remembered the long rambling conversations we used to have. I'd taken him in – or, to be more precise, had let him stay in Titus's place when the old man was in hospital.

One day he vanished as unexpectedly as he'd appeared, leaving behind his manuscript about the moon – and that was the last that was known of him. I could find no trace of him on Facebook and not even on LinkedIn, because it was ages since Valdemar had had a job.

Lost in combat.

Is that how things were going to end up with Gabriela? The fact that we hadn't lived together had the advantage that I had nothing belonging to her in my flat, except for a vase which no longer existed. Whether she came back from Paris or not, she might also disappear from my life.

Trying to keep these dismal thoughts at bay, I answered Daniel Lumbreras's long letter. My mood wasn't exactly lyrical, but I told him how much I liked his email and that I wanted to go to one of his concerts one day.

After I sent my email, the hollowness and the loneliness took over my bedroom even more forcefully.

That was when I remembered Meritxell. Apart from the fact that she'd been Mishima's vet ever since I'd found him – and he was already halfway through his feline life – we had a relationship that was something like a low-key friendship.

We hadn't spoken for almost a year, but I decided to call her without worrying too much about inventing an excuse. As if he could read the number I was calling, Mishima jumped off the bed and slunk out of the room.

"Hello, is that you, Samuel?"

"Yes." I wasn't sure whether that was still true or not. "It's far too long since I brought Mishima in for a check-up."

"Is there anything wrong with him?"

"Not as far as I know..." I hastened to add: "Well, he's been scratching his ear a lot lately. Perhaps we need to make sure he hasn't got fleas or something like that."

"If he's scratching a lot, take him to the centre, but I won't be able to treat him," she said in her usual forthright way. "I can't touch cats for a while. Health reasons."

"Does that mean you're not working?"

"Not right now."

Then I realized how absurd this conversation was. You're a real loser if you need to go to your cat's vet for a bit of human kindness. But Meritxell suddenly said, "I'm actually very close to your place now. I've come to Gràcia to do some shopping. Do you want..."

I interrupted her. "Yes, let's have coffee."

"OK. I'll see you at Café Canigó. I've got big news for you."

A Surprising Invitation

It was ten past five in the afternoon when I met Meritxell at the door of one of Gràcia's old cafés, cooled by fans whirring from its high ceiling. I immediately spotted the nature of her big news.

A very prominent belly announced the advanced stage of her pregnancy. Otherwise she was still the serene woman with lovely features I'd met eight years earlier. She smiled as if amused by my surprise at her state.

"Congratulations," I said, kissing her on each cheek. "I didn't know..."

"I didn't know either a year ago. But that's what happened – sort of all of a sudden."

As we went to sit down, I told myself I must be very thick, because I didn't understand what she was trying to tell me. Embracing Titus's new habit, I asked for green tea before saying teasingly, "All of a sudden? You make it sound as easy as getting a mushroom to pop up in a pot."

Meritxell laughed at my silliness, which gave me a chance to admire the harmony of her features. There was something about her that gave out a sense of peace, which was probably helped by her deep yet sweet voice.

"I'm not with anyone," she blurted out. "This boy will have to grow up without a father."

I was surprised by her spontaneous confession. Pouring tea into my cup, I plucked up the courage to ask, "Did the baby's father leave you?"

"I don't know who he is." Once again, she seemed to find my reaction amusing. "I opted for artificial insemination."

I tasted my tea – which was not nearly as good as Titus's – thinking that Meritxell was braver than I'd thought. I now understood what she'd said about being off work. Pregnant women are usually advised to keep away from cats.

She took a sip of her mineral water and went on, "I'm nearly forty and I got tired of waiting for the man I'd want to settle down and have a family with. After a few let-downs I decided to make my dream come true all by myself."

"You'll be a great mother."

"I'll do my best. I don't know my little boy yet, but I already love him so much I'm sure I'll cope."

"It could be tough at first…" I mused aloud. "What about when the baby's four months old and you've got to go back to work? Are you close to your family?"

"I don't have a family. My parents were quite old when I was born, and they died a while ago. I have no brothers or sisters."

"In that case, I admire you even more. There are plenty of terrified future fathers and mothers who have lots of family around them."

Meritxell rewarded me with a smile that lit up her eyes. Then she asked me how I was. I didn't hide anything from her, but didn't go into details either. Neither did she try to pry into the reasons for my separation, for which I was grateful, because I didn't know myself.

Like Titus, she seemed fascinated about the matter of the two postcards and gave me the same advice. "If I were you, I'd go looking for this nameless friend."

"But I don't know who's sending me these postcards. I only know that they're coming from Kyoto." Then I told her about the handwritten words *wabi-sabi* and what they meant.

"The old capital of Japan," she sighed. "I've always wanted to go there. It takes time to get round to doing these things... And you don't have the sender's address either?"

"I don't think so, though I discovered that the first post-card – the one with the waving cat – has the address of a workshop on the back."

"A workshop where they make *maneki-nekos*?"

"No, I don't think so... These cats come from China. It says *atelier*. Maybe it has something to do with *wabi-sabi*. Or maybe not. How would I know?"

"Go there and ask if someone from that workshop sent them."

"That's crazy! I don't know anyone there, and I don't understand how this person's got my address."

"All the more reason for going there. Didn't you say your holidays start in a couple of weeks?"

"You talk as if Kyoto was just around the corner," I muttered. Now, for the first time, I pondered playing along with this madness. "The flight there must take fifteen or sixteen hours."

"That wouldn't be so different from when you're sitting at home reading," she prodded. "You won't notice the time. Just make sure you're here in August."

"Well, I have to be back at the faculty then..." I was surprised. "Why did you say that?"

"Well, actually I feel a bit embarrassed about this." Her eyes wandered to the glass door through which we could see the Plaça de la Revolució bathed in afternoon sunlight. "Would you like to be my son's godfather?"

Preparations for a Journey

I spent the next few days in a mood that swung erratically from sadness to perplexity with some flashes of hope in between. The hope was nourished by Meritxell's unexpected invitation, which I'd accepted without knowing why.

Well, in fact I did know: in the depths of the existential abyss into which I'd plunged – to land at the gateway to depression – I thought that the fact that a single mum had asked me to be godfather to her baby was, at the very least, a beautiful idea.

Yes, she was only my cat's vet, and we hadn't seen each other for a year, but it was comforting to know that in a few weeks somebody, somewhere, would be waiting for me.

Then again, while I was trying to digest the fact that Gabriela had left me, everything that reminded me of her – even my own city – hurt me.

I was a creature of habit, and going back to my solitary man's routine was like stepping onto a minefield. Everywhere I went was somewhere I'd been with her.

She'd often come to the faculty with me after spending the night at my place. We'd walked up and down Carrer Verdi a thousand times, to have a glass of wine at La Baignoire, browse among the books in Taifa, or dive into the Verdi cinema to see some art-house film. Now everything in my world was reminding me that she'd gone.

The idea that I needed to sort my head out, however ridiculous the way of going about it, was taking shape. Why not go to Kyoto? Titus and Meritxell said I should, even though I didn't know where to find the *wabi-sabi* workshop.

Even Daniel Lumbreras had disappeared after that long email of his.

Alone and with a long summer ahead, I really did need a change of scene. The old city of Kyoto seemed as good a place as any.

My mind immediately went to work on the logistics. All those years of Germanic influence were not in vain. The Japanese consulate informed me I didn't need any kind of visa as long as my stay in the country didn't exceed ninety days.

I contacted a Japanese tourist office, which talked me into buying a two-week ticket to travel around the country on the *Shinkansen* – even though I'd had no intention whatsoever of engaging in bullet-train tourism. They also organized an extremely expensive four-day stay at a *ryokan*, one of Kyoto's traditional hostels.

I got an open-return ticket with Qatar Airways, via Doha. A Lonely Planet guide to Japan completed my travelling kit.

Once I had everything neatly piled on my writing desk at home, I realized there was one more detail to be seen to. Who was going to look after Mishima while I was in the country that had given him his name?

The answer was upstairs.

It was Sunday by the time I got around to going up to tell Titus I was leaving, and that he'd have the cat sitting under his train-set table for a couple of weeks. I didn't think I'd last much longer in such an unfamiliar, different country.

The door opened with its usual buzz. As I walked down the passageway where the *Wanderer above the Sea of Fog* was hanging, the machine-gun rattling of

Titus's keyboard told me that he was well into his *wabi-sabi* book.

"*Konnichiwa*," I greeted him, using the first words I'd learnt from the list of useful expressions in my guide.

"Good afternoon! I'm happy to see that you've finally made up your mind."

"I've got to get out of Barcelona for a while."

"You don't need excuses. The trip will be good for you, and I have a sneaking suspicion that you're going to discover something important."

I moved a couple of collections of aphorisms so I could sit on the stool beside him. Titus usually printed out and corrected his work at the end of the day: judging by the pile of paper next to his computer, the book was proceeding apace.

"If you need anything from Japan, I imagine I'll have plenty of time to find it."

"Let's see about that. The way time behaves in Kyoto is still a big unknown. As Einstein said, time is relative, but subject to movement and space."

"You sound as if I was about to board a rocket bound for another planet."

Titus raised his glasses on his forehead and gave me a grave look. “I’d say that’s a pretty good description of what this journey of yours is going to be like.”

KYOTO

The Death of Yukio Mishima

When the plane took off, the whole thing seemed like magic. It wasn't just that this heavy lump of metal had managed to defy gravity: the fact that a sedentary guy like me, with no relationship with Japan, should have set out on this journey because of a couple of postcards was what really made me think I was under some sort of spell.

I was sitting next to a girl who'd dolled up her chador with what seemed to be very expensive high heels. She soon started playing a virtual golf game on the screen in front of her seat, while I alternated between jotting down notes and reading a novel.

Titus had asked me to bring him three little-known varieties of tea and also to find out everything I could about *wabi-sabi*. He'd only managed to get his hands on three or four books, which offered very little information about the beauty of imperfection.

Using the name of Gottfried Kerstin, the old man didn't just want to meet the terms of his contract with his small self-help publisher.

"I want to publish the most complete book ever written on *wabi-sabi*. So I need you to get me some original material. If I manage to get it published in other languages, I'll give you a share of my earnings."

I told him there was no need for that, and that I'd be really happy to help him in exchange for his looking after Mishima, but he insisted that we were partners in this venture. He'd even given me three books from his library after he'd scanned the chapters that interested him into his computer.

Flying towards Doha, however, I wasn't yet ready to immerse myself in a world that is imperfect, ephemeral and unfinished. My life was shaky enough as it was.

Instead of reading Titus's books, I opened a novel by Murakami which I wanted to read again – *A Wild Sheep Chase*. This was his first book to be published in Catalan. I thought it was a masterpiece, but it was still almost totally unknown.

The story begins by recalling the life of the main character in the early Seventies.

As he and his girlfriend are out on a walk, they start bickering over the silliest matters, as tends to happen when, for whatever baffling reason, a relationship begins to fall apart.

She tells him about a recurrent nightmare in which a vending machine keeps eating her change.

In the middle of this trivial conversation, Murakami brings the story back to the deep magic of old Japanese legends and talks about birds flying off, swallowed up into the cloudless sky, as the girl draws indecipherable patterns in the dirt with a twig. This is where his greatness lies: in his ability to mix humdrum details that seem to be leading nowhere with sublime touches. At one point the girl tells the narrator:

"Sometimes I get real lonely sleeping with you."

I was shaken by these words, because they stirred up something I'd often felt with Gabriela: the feeling that, for some mysterious reason, she was moving away from me – usually after we'd made love. The sex was great but, once she'd come, she'd just lie there staring at the ceiling. If I asked her what she was thinking about, she said: "Nothing." Which was probably true.

I kept reading on.

The day of Yukio Mishima's death something died for that couple in my book, but they couldn't understand what had happened.

The Last Earthquake in Tokyo

I wasn't prepared for our arrival in Doha airport. I'd slept twenty minutes at the most, and the early hour and a blast of more than forty degrees left me completely stupefied.

What was supposed to be a great modern airport with hundreds of connections was still unfinished, so we had to squeeze into a shuttle bus to cover the interminable distance between where we'd stopped on the runway to the Far East departures terminal.

There, I mingled with a horde of besuited executives, fashion victims and djellaba-clad travellers as I went through passport control once again. My flight was leaving in a couple of hours, so I wandered off to look for the Tokyo-Narita departure gate.

I was so tired I could barely hold my head up. I couldn't wait to sit down on the plane again, cramped though it was. I needed to close my eyes.

I wanted to get something to drink at the bar, but there was a long queue and only one barman, who was working flat out to meet the demand for cappuccinos. Meanwhile, in the luxury boutiques, there were two assistants for every customer.

I availed myself of the airport's free Internet access to check the news on my smartphone. I gave up when I read that a Russian bank was recommending that people who can't pay their debts should commit suicide. There was a great hue and cry over this, which prompted one of the directors to claim that it was a joke to scare customers who hadn't repaid their debts and refused to respond to the bank's attempts to contact them.

I was about to go back to my Murakami novel when the man sitting next to me decided he wanted to have a chat. His suntan and dyed blond hair made him look like your typical ageing English (or so I judged from his accent) misfit.

"Business or pleasure?"

I was about to say "Neither", but that would have required too much explanation. "Documentation. I'm writing a book about *wabi-sabi* with a friend, and I have to do a few interviews in order to finish it."

"Wasabi?" He was very surprised. "Well of course you need to mix it with your soya sauce so you can dip your sushi in it, but I'd never have thought you could write a book about it."

"I'm sure there must be books about Japanese horseradish," I said, "but *wabi-sabi* is another matter."

Since he didn't ask me what *wabi-sabi* was, that looked like the end of the conversation. However, after my two lonely weeks, I had a sudden urge to talk, so I asked: "And what about you? Why are you going to Tokyo?"

"I work in Tokyo, in a language academy. You can't imagine how difficult it is to teach English in that place. They're nearly as thick as the people in your country."

I was offended by this oblique reference to my bad pronunciation. After all, I was a lecturer in Germanic Philology. Anyway, I said, "What's it like living in Japan?"

"Quite comfortable for a *gaijin*. The students respect us, Japanese women are fascinated by us and life's pretty sweet if you don't mind the pollution and radiation from Fukushima."

"Oh yes, of course..." I'd forgotten about the nuclear disaster. Now worried, I asked, "And how are they managing that?"

"Quite well. The proof is that, despite everything, they got the Olympic Games. The Japanese have known how to live with catastrophe since they lost the war. As for me, as soon as I arrived in the country, there was a magnitude 7 earthquake. I was on the twentieth floor of an office building where I'd gone to teach a bunch of businessmen. I really thought that was curtains."

The man was a good storyteller. His students must have liked him.

"The skyscraper swayed from side to side like a metronome needle. Without moving from where I was, I could see different parts of Tokyo as I waited for the building to split in two and send us flying into space."

"So what happened?"

"The building remained standing. They make them flexible and with very deep foundations. They're well prepared." The man was proud of his country of adoption. "Well, actually, there was no transport for a few days. People had to walk kilometres to get to work. Some slept in the office because they didn't want to waste working hours."

"That's admirable."

"It certainly is! But you'll never guess what the collateral damage was."

I remained silent while he fixed me with a weary wolfish gaze before delivering the punchline.

"The whole city ran out of toilet paper in a couple of hours. You couldn't get it in any shop in Tokyo."

"Why?"

"Because everyone rushed out to stock up," he said. "But not because they were shitting themselves. They remembered the previous earthquake and the problems of supply caused by that..."

Waiting for Mount Fuji

After getting through passport control at Tokyo Narita Airport, I lost my bearings for a few minutes until someone showed me where to find the underground railway platform for my train to Kyoto. I'd just discovered that English is as little known in Japan as Japanese is to Catalans.

I stepped into an aseptic office and validated my rail pass. Then I went off to get my *Shinkansen,* which bypassed Tokyo and required one change along the way.

Once settled in my window seat, I took one of Titus's books about *wabi-sabi* from my bag.

> *Wabi-sabi* aesthetics is highly melancholic and autumnal. It is an aesthetics which works with organic materials that age with use and, somehow, have their own lives: wood, hemp, rusty metal, rough-woven cloth, ceramics. Surfaces do not need to be polished, trim and regular but, rather, they should be wrinkled, imperfect and unfinished.

Things aren't permanent, but are condemned to disappear or be transformed, and this imbues them with melancholy charm.

It was difficult to think about that beautifully imperfect world in a railway carriage rushing along straight tracks. When it started to run above ground, however, I began to see that *wabi-sabi* is also present in modernity, although in a less poetic form.

The territory between Narita and the immense conurbation of the Greater Tokyo Area, home to some thirty-five million people, is a succession of soulless, higgledy-piggledy neighbourhoods in which most of the buildings are vertical cubicles with antennae, making them look like strange, man-made insects.

Beyond the endless strip of buildings it is possible to glimpse the countryside and mountains in the background.

I'd read once that, in this country, the change from city to unpopulated rural land is dramatic. The Japanese are a gregarious people and like to live clustered together. Very few are attracted by the idea of living in an isolated house in the midst of nature.

Hence, once the bullet train has left behind the ring roads of cities, another Japan begins, with cultivated fields and expanses of green that make it hard to believe that this is a nation with a population of one hundred and thirty million.

After changing trains, I was watching out for Mount Fuji and its perpetually snowy peak. My guidebook informed me that we would be passing quite close to it on the way to Old Kyoto. This was an image that was etched on my mind thanks to a series of childhood comic books, and I was hoping to see it before nightfall blotted out the landscape.

The train was due to arrive at nine fifteen. Although I'd slept very little on the plane, I was too excited to nod off on the train. I divided my time between looking at the views outside, Titus's book and the other passengers in the carriage.

Nearly all of them were tapping out messages on their smartphones or watching films on their iPads. The men were impeccably dressed, and every single woman looked as if she'd just stepped out of the hairdresser's. My first impression of the people of Japan was one of extreme neatness and discretion.

At no point did I catch anyone looking at me, although I was the only *gaijin* in the carriage. Everyone seemed to be absorbed with his or her own affairs as if the world beyond didn't exist.

The golden light of evening fell broodingly over increasingly more disperse groups of buildings and houses surrounded by crops and hills, which preannounced the appearance of the legendary mountain.

In a moment of weakness I wished that Gabriela was sitting beside me enjoying these evanescent views. Sharing the beauty of things that elude us and disappear. Like her.

My fellow passengers in the *Shinkansen* suddenly looked up from their screens to gaze out of the windows. They pointed their cameras and mobiles in the same direction, waiting to capture the peak we'd all been longing to see.

A tear rolled down my cheek as I contemplated the eternal presence of Mount Fuji, transmitting the serenity of an all-seeing, all-understanding giant.

Kyoto

At first sight, Kyoto was very different from what I'd expected. The one thousand six hundred temples featured in the Lonely Planet guide seemed to be a long way from the prodigious metal architecture of the railway station with its gleaming roof and lifts leading endlessly upwards to high boutique-lined walkways.

Dizzy with the sheer size of this hangar which, at that hour of night, was swarming with people, I took a few minutes to get outside. A retro-modern TV antenna near the taxi rank looked as if it would be more at home in East Berlin than in the city of Japan's ancient essences.

I got into a taxi that was impeccable inside and outside, with white lace covers on the seats and even the steering wheel. When I showed the driver the address of the Blue Frogs (yes, that was the translation of the Japanese name) *ryokan* which I was booked into, he nodded respectfully and the car glided away smoothly.

I was disappointed to find that the streets were lined by the same kind of modern buildings I'd seen from the train:

functional blocks of some ten or twelve storeys at most. If it wasn't for the flashing signs written in kanji, anyone might think this was a small American city. Indeed, the old imperial capital has a smaller population than Barcelona.

The extreme looks flaunted by some kids in the streets and the glittery designs of video arcades shooting out bright flares to the sound of deafening techno-beat only confirmed my impression that there was no Zen in Kyoto that Wednesday night.

The taxi turned off the main thoroughfare to enter an alley where another city began. We'd gone back five centuries. Lanterns hanging from two-storey buildings lit up a paved footpath where couples strolled. Some wore traditional dress – the women in delicate kimonos and clog-like sandals, the men in body-hugging silk robes tied at the waist.

A luxury car stopped in front of us, blocking the way. A geisha got out and, in a moment, slipped inside a tea house – an astounding sight that made me wonder if I was hallucinating. Not long afterwards, we drew up in front of the *ryokan*.

At most, the hostel had seven or eight rooms distributed over the two floors of a wooden house with bamboo blinds. The sign was also made of wood. Although the name was written in Japanese, the blue frogs painted on it confirmed that this was the right place.

I paid my fare – the equivalent of around twenty euros – and the silent driver used some automatic device to open the door and let me out.

A woman who was barely five feet tall peeped out from behind one of the blinds and came to greet me. She beckoned me inside and went to stand beside a piece of wooden furniture that looked more like a dressing table than a reception desk.

Some white slippers awaited me inside the door. I took off my shoes, and the woman made a deep bow saying, "*Irasshaimase…*", which I took to be some kind of welcome.

I gave her my passport and reservation document. As she painstakingly wrote my name in a clothbound book, I asked if I might have something to eat.

The lady's startled expression showed that she didn't understand a word of English. She led me up to the first floor and pushed open a sliding door to show me my austere accommodation, which consisted of a low futon, an equally low bedside table, a wardrobe and a small bathroom. And that was all. One hundred and eighty euros a night. Maybe I was paying for the location of the place in the old city.

It was now half past ten and I hadn't eaten anything since landing at Narita mid-afternoon. After a quick shower with lukewarm water, I got changed, ready to go looking for a bite to eat in that dreamlike alley.

The distant notes of something that sounded like a lute and a girl singing reminded me of the geisha I'd seen getting out of the car. I wondered if I'd get to see another geisha or whether I'd just been lucky to see that one.

I was surprised to realize that, for the first time since I'd sunk into my depression, I wanted something. That was heartening.

The Mushroom Song

The Japanese couples I'd seen from the taxi had now vanished from the alley. All it had to show now were closed shops, a couple of *ryokans* and the occasional, hopeful glow of a street light.

As I walked through this small world of modest houses, I glimpsed human silhouettes on the ground floor, shadows gracefully gliding around inside them, flitting across blinds and paper screens. I wondered whether one of them might have belonged to the geisha, now plying her arts in a private tea house.

The voice and lute I'd heard only minutes earlier were silent now.

Just when I was starting to fear I'd have to return to my futon with an empty stomach I saw, inscribed on an iron plaque lit by the sallow glow from a lamp post, three Latin-script letters that left no room for doubt: BAR.

I pushed open the black door.

On the other side was a tiny room of less than ten square metres with an L-shaped bar that would have accommodated four customers at the most. Behind the bar, a wizened woman in her sixties bowed slightly and gestured at one of the empty stools. At the other end of the L, an elderly man was enthralled by an almost-empty bottle of sake.

As if trying to snap him out of his stupor, the woman went to top up his ceramic cup with what remained in the bottle, and the man nodded. He looked so eccentric it was difficult to guess his age. He was wearing a pin-striped suit and tie; his hair was tousled and his glasses scratched. He peered at me for a moment, as if trying to work out what I was doing there. Then he went back to contemplating his sake.

An old television set with a twenty-inch screen hung aslant from the ceiling, showing music videos of stridently rendered songs and images that looked like some kind of joke but were serious.

I was offered the list of house specialties with another bow. To my great relief, each item – basically different kinds of sake, beer and cocktails – had an English translation written beneath its Japanese name. Nothing to eat except little trays of nuts coming with the drinks.

Knowing I'd probably get drunk on an empty stomach, I asked for an astronomically priced Asahi: nine hundred yen, almost seven euros. As the woman filled my glass with the chilled beer, the man with the scratched glasses suddenly stood up and burst into song.

Astounded, I saw that he had picked up a wireless microphone to sing along with the show that now appeared on the screen, consisting of a dance performed by children dressed up as mushrooms. The woman turned up the volume so that the man could belt it out, backed by the syncopated beat of chords that sounded like traditional Russian music. The vocal part was very repetitive and kitsch, especially coming from that executive who looked as if he'd just escaped from a catfight.

Dokonoko no kinoko kono kinoko dokono
dokonoko no kinoko morino kinoko
morino kinoko wa rappa ni natte
onpu ga kumo made tondetta

puppuru pappa purupappa
puppuru pappa purupappa
sora niwa naisho no hanashi dayo

Some notes were too high for this oddball, who was totally unfazed by his inability to hold a tune. The bar owner listened to him with her arms crossed, apparently pleased by this little show for an audience of two.

I was dismayed to discover that I'd inadvertently wandered into a karaoke bar for the lonely.

After a ridiculous polka-beat climax, the grey-haired man sat down again, dignified, though with the expression of someone lost in some very murky musings.

I picked up a handful of nuts to take the edge off my hunger before having a sip of my beer. I felt like a fish out of water. Just then he asked in fairly comprehensible English, "You do not know that song?"

Okamura

As I would soon find out, it wasn't easy to find English speakers in Japan. I answered politely without suspecting that the lonesome karaoke star was going to become my shadow every night – a key character in my Japanese story.

"No, I don't know it," I confessed without leaving my corner of the L. "In fact, I've only just arrived in the country."

"That explains it, then." He smiled. "You will not find anyone here who does not know 'Dokonoko no Kinoko'."

"It sounds like a tongue-twister."

"It is a children's song, but it's very popular with adults too. Many people have it as a ringtone on their mobile phones. We have even a 'Dokonoko no Kinoko' dance."

I finished my beer. Thank Heavens the Japanese gentleman didn't get up from his stool to do the dance. I would have got an attack of the giggles.

For the sake of saying something, I told him, "I've never been in a karaoke bar. I usually listen to classical music."

"Me too." He pulled a face as if I'd offended him. "The Russians – especially Tchaikovsky and all composers after him until Prokofiev. I have not interest in the music that came later."

Marvelling at the discovery that the karaoke man loved the great Russian composers, I couldn't resist asking, "So how come you decided to sing a modern kids' song?"

"Therapy." He smiled timidly, then drained the last drop from his glass. "For depression. My wife, she died not a year ago and the doctor tells me it is good way to get distract my mind. I come here after work and, if I want to, I sing a song. To not have fear of look ridiculous is good for head. I strongly recommend for you to try it."

"I couldn't even if I wanted to." I was afraid he'd ask the woman to put on another song. "My knowledge of Japanese is zero, except for a couple of words."

"My niece, she will transcribe the words so you can read them. The tunes are easy. They are catchy like mushroom song."

"The mushroom song? Ah, you mean that song about *kino*..."

"'Dokonoko no Kinoko'," he repeated. "It is about adventures of a mushroom in the forest. By the way, my name is Okamura. I am sorry I do not have card with me."

He bowed formally, and I imitated him without getting up from my stool. The woman was staring at my empty glass, waiting for me to ask for another beer. But all of a sudden I was overwhelmed with tiredness.

I put nine hundred yen on the bar. The woman took a step backwards and, shaking her head, gave me a shocked look. Then she got a biro and wrote some large numbers on a piece of paper: 1,400.

I picked up her drinks list and indignantly pointed at the price marked for my beer. She responded with hand flapping and head shaking, but I didn't understand what she was trying to tell me until Okamura intervened.

"She put cover charge for first drink. All small bars they open at night do this."

I took a five-hundred-yen note from my wallet and put it on the bar. Even its picture of Mount Fuji didn't stop me from feeling pissed off. More than ten euros for a beer in a dive with a drunk who sang about a mushroom in a forest seemed really over the top.

Okamura saw how irked I was and murmured, "This is first thing you must remember when you go to drink. In Japan, smaller bar mean bigger prices."

Less is more. I remembered the maxim that kept cropping up in Titus's books.

"It is totally logical," Okamura went on. "The lady of this establishment which can fit few customers has to do same as the big bar. Life it cost same price for everyone."

I was ashamed of getting worked up about the ten euros. After all, the lady, who was now washing my glass, had had very meagre takings that Wednesday night. If I wasn't in such a state of stupefaction from lack of sleep, I would have asked for another beer.

"Thank you for telling me, Mr Okamura." I took my leave.

"Don't worry. Many people, they go to bigger places for no be hit by surcharge, but they will not find what has this place."

"You mean the karaoke?"

"No! There is karaoke everywhere. We two we meet here. That is the good thing. Next time I come with my niece. She speak perfect English and she will be happy to meet you. In fact, she is my English teacher, two times a week."

I bowed before leaving the bar, wrongly convinced that there would be no next time.

"What's the name of the bar?" I asked, purely out of courtesy. "It might be difficult to find if I come again some night."

"It does not have name yet. The owner only came one week ago and she does not like old name. Do you have suggestion?"

I shrugged, the best answer I could come up with, before going out into the silence of the night. The moon shone down on the cobbled lane in old Kyoto, promising adventures. A casual encounter in a nameless bar was just the beginning.

Wabi & Sabi

Although I'd gone to bed after midnight, tired after my long journey, jet lag opened my eyes at four in the morning. I was wide awake.

My body's alarm clock had gone off, and there was no way it was going to let me go back to sleep. Lying on my bone-achingly hard mattress, I tried for quite a while to fight it, but to no avail. Finally, acknowledging defeat, I got up.

It was a quarter to five when I picked up one of Titus's essays, thinking I could read it in the *onsen*, the thermal bath offered by every *ryokan*.

In dressing gown and slippers, and equipped with towel and book, I went downstairs to the ground floor and the *onsen*. Unsurprisingly, at that hour there was nobody else in the place, which seemed to have been carved out of the rocky subsoil. It was a natural pool facing a window looking out onto a chaotic, overgrown garden. On one side, two taps were set into the wall, with metal buckets placed beneath them.

I understood that I had to wash myself before getting into the yellowish *onsen* water. I stripped off while waiting for the bucket to fill, after which I poured it over my head. The icy water was like an electric shock. Then I quickly stepped into the natural pool with the book in my hand. The water was pleasantly warm.

Now seated on a flat underwater rock, I gave my attention to the concept which, ten thousand kilometres away, was taking up so much of Titus's time and efforts.

As a philologist, I couldn't overlook the origins of the word, so I started with that. It seems that *sabi* was originally used to describe the subtle, somewhat sombre and tenebrous beauty of twelfth- and thirteenth-century Japanese poetry. Titus's anthology informed me that the word summoned up wistful feelings, something like a "sparrow foraging in a pile of fallen autumn leaves".

According to the book, the other part of the equation, the word *wabi*, conjured up humility and austerity, the refined poverty born of indifference towards wealth and ostentation.

Fascinated by this sophisticated sentiment, I flipped through the pages looking for separate descriptions of the two terms. Kamo no Chomei, a hermit monk who lived at the end of the twelfth and early thirteenth centuries, said:

> *Wabi* is what we feel when contemplating a twilight sky in autumn, the wistfulness of the colour when all sound is silenced, those moments when, for some inexplicable reason, unstoppable tears start to fall.

Lounging in the water of the *onsen*, I recalled for the umpteenth time David Friedrich's painting hanging in Titus's hallway. Everything about that man standing on a mountain was melancholy.

I wondered whether this was the sentiment that inspired the haikus and watercolours by Japanese artists. Perhaps they had another way of experiencing the beauty of what we can't retain.

Is there such a thing as universal melancholy?

Immersed in the sulphurous water, I was recovering my essence of the romantic man who shoos away solitude with such questions. A distraction, like any other.

There was a second definition of *wabi*, this time offered by a present-day author, Makoto Ueda, Professor Emeritus of Japanese Literature at Stanford University. For him:

> *Wabi* is the beauty that springs from the creative energy that flows in all things, animate or not. It is a kind of beauty that, like nature itself, can appear with darkness

> and light, and be sad and joyful, rough and gentle. The beauty of this force of nature is imperfect, always changing and beyond our reach.

Before I could ponder this text, a very large Japanese man came into the *onsen* and threw a bucket of cold water over himself in stoic silence. He then lumbered over to the pool with a towel draped around his neck.

"*Ohayōgozaimasu.*"

I understood that, with this muttered greeting, he was wishing me good morning. It was half past five, and the business-trip guests in the *ryokan* were starting to stir.

As if the warm water was healing deep, long-open wounds, the man grunted with pleasure a couple of times.

The Japanese tend to share public space as if they are alone, but I felt uncomfortable sharing that natural pool with this colossus. Once again, the book came to my rescue. Professor Ueda now brought the two words *wabi* and *sabi* together.

> *Wabi* originally meant "sadness of poverty". But gradually it came to mean an attitude towards life with which one tried to resign himself to straitened living and to find peace and serenity of mind even under such

circumstances. *Sabi*, primarily an aesthetic concept, is closely related to *wabi*, a philosophical idea.

My academic's brain – which had revelled in the classes I'd taken in aesthetics and history of thought – couldn't ignore this provocative blending of meaning which I was still far from understanding.

I didn't get out of the pool in the small spa until my skin was totally wrinkled. Another bucket of icy water completed the cure.

I was ready for my first morning in Kyoto.

Good Times with Older Dogs

Breakfast in the *ryokan* took the form of rice and fish, served at such low tables that anyone wanting to sit down had to be a yoga expert. That dish, first thing in the morning, might have looked very strange if I'd not gone to bed without dinner.

I got up from the table with backache. Before setting out to explore Kyoto, I looked up the address of the atelier in my Lonely Planet guide – not that I really hoped I'd glean any information about the mysterious postcard sender who'd brought me all the way to Japan.

And then, what did a production-line porcelain cat have to do with the organic philosophy of *wabi-sabi*?

Answer: nothing.

An old armchair gave some support to my back. On one side was a magazine rack offering several publications in Japanese and, on the other, three shelves with books on different subjects in several languages.

It seemed they'd been left there by visitors to the *ryokan* who'd read them and didn't want to lug them around any more. There was only one book in English, and the title was so odd that I couldn't resist taking it down from the shelf.

GOOD TIMES WITH OLDER DOGS

The cover showed two patient, weary-looking dogs with grizzled muzzles. I could almost hear their hoarse, muted barking, trying in vain to scare someone who was venturing too close to their house.

The book was written for an American readership, and I checked out the back cover to get an idea of what it was about. It described the pleasures of living with old dogs after many years of coexistence. The animal has less energy and is less demanding, but makes up for it with deeper understanding of its owner's changing psychology.

It was very *wabi-sabi*.

If the dog's owner is elderly too, I thought, dog and owner would eventually reach the stage when they'd end up resembling each other – not only in their way of hobbling around, but also in their expressions.

I returned the book to its place on the shelf, thinking that my old age would be worse than that of those mute old dogs. They at least had someone to follow round and love. Apart from a cat that did what it pleased and would live ten more years at the most, I was all alone in the world.

This upsetting thought made me connect my phone to the *ryokan*'s Wi-Fi network.

WhatsApp showed I'd received two messages since the last time I'd connected in Doha.

The first one, to my great surprise, was from Daniel Lumbreras. I'd forgotten that I'd given him my mobile number when I'd written to him. His message was to the point.

I'm in Gràcia. Shall we meet for coffee? DANIEL.

I answered that I would have loved to have coffee with him, but was too far away to get to my neighbourhood at a reasonable hour. I finished by saying I'd contact him when I got back and opened the second message. Seeing that it was from Gabriela, I read it with apprehension.

Dear Samuel,
Titus told me you've gone to Tokyo. Nice idea. I wouldn't worry re trying to find sender of postcards. This person will find you if he wants to. xxxx GABRIELA.

The Mysterious Address

My first daylight stroll around Kyoto led me into the traditional streets of the Gion district where my *ryokan* was located. Some businesses were open, and several antiques and clothing shops, and small cafes and restaurants were already showing signs of life.

Wandering around this area, I came to the narrow Pontocho Street, which runs parallel to the Kamo River. Walking past tea houses and clubs with a covert air, even in broad daylight, I wondered whether the *wabi-sabi* workshop was in this part of the city.

I was still dazed after my journey and had forgotten to ask about it at the *ryokan*, but I had the evidence I needed with me: the postcards.

I leant against a tree that had sprung out of the paving stones like a mushroom. On the back of the cat postcard, the blue ink of the words *wabi-sabi* seemed to glow in a special way.

I peered at the tiny words that seemed to be connected with the workshop. They were followed by some kanji characters and the number twenty-seven, so I imagined that must have been its address. I then started examining the Golden Pavilion postcard. Apart from my name, nothing was written on it, and there was no address. The only clue was in the postmark, which was the same on both postcards: a quarter of a circle with the same kanji characters and a four-figure number below it: 4,032. That might mean they'd been posted in the same district.

They may have had the same postmark, but the two peculiar stamps couldn't have been more different. One showed an Akita (a breed of dog I recognized because I'd seen Richard Gere's film *Hachi*), complete with curly tail and radiant halo. The other showed four women in mauve tunics standing next to an old telescope. One was looking through it while two others observed her with interest and the fourth was gazing at the sky as if she trusted her own eyes more than the instrument.

In the bottom left-hand corner of both stamps there was an inscription saying *NIPPON 820*. I realized that was what the stamp cost – just over six euros.

While I was wondering about all this, a woman of around sixty stopped in front of me. Dressed in a skirt and jacket, she bowed courteously and then held out her hand to take the postcard I was staring at – the one that had the workshop's address. It seemed she wanted to help, so I gratefully handed it to her, making a small bow in return. Behind the very thick lenses of her glasses, her considerably magnified eyes opened wide in astonishment when she read it. As if Satan himself had jumped out of that address, she hastily returned the postcard, bowed once more and scurried off down the street.

I was left standing there wondering what kind of place this workshop must be if it scared the woman so much. Curiosity made me scan the host of Japanese people filling Pontocho Street at this early hour of the morning to see if I could identify someone who might speak English. I wanted to know where the postcard was going to lead me.

I chose a long-haired boy who was carrying a folder covered with pictures of the Sex Pistols and went over to him.

"Excuse me, can you tell me the district where I might find this address?"

The boy took the postcard, leading me to believe he'd understood me. But he handed it back a couple of seconds later with an uneasy smile.

"What's going on with this place?" I was more and more bewildered.

"Sorry, I can't tell you." He shrugged and rushed away, still clutching his folder.

Nothing Has Existed or Will Exist for Ever

I thought that this startling reaction from two such different people might mean that the Japanese are wary about giving directions to a foreigner because they don't want to risk your getting lost if they don't know the address. The workshop must have been in one of Kyoto's back streets or in an industrial estate on the outskirts of the city.

That was the most reasonable theory I could come up with, but the taxi driver I stopped just as he was leaving Pontocho Street added a third degree of weirdness to the matter of the address. He stuck his head out of the window and took the postcard. When I pointed at the address, he put on his glasses to read the small print.

Two seconds later, I was standing there holding the postcard while the taxi driver was flapping his hand in a way that clearly said no. Before I could even ask why he didn't want to take me, he drove off leaving me more nonplussed than ever.

I wandered back to the *ryokan*, pensive and with my hands in my pockets. *So this isn't an address that people don't know. Everyone knows what this place is and what happens there. It must be a really awful place if it scares a taxi driver and a guy who listens to the Sex Pistols.*

Cocooned in overpowering drowsiness, I came up with all sorts of implausible theories: it could be an infamous brothel, or an *onsen* where the bosses of the *yakuza* mafia meet, or even a nuclear-waste storage site of questionable security.

These were extreme – even absurd – possibilities, which left me even more in the dark about who had sent me the postcards. To cap it all off, just before I entered the *ryokan*, a black cat shot past me. I dismissed all premonitions of bad luck by reminding myself of what Groucho Marx said: "If a black cat crosses your path, it means that the animal is going somewhere."

As I walked past the reception desk, I was about to show the tiny woman the address on my postcard, but in the end I didn't. If that *atelier* was some degenerate kind of place, she might call the police and then I'd have problems explaining how I'd come to receive the postcards. Yes, it was best not to ask. On my first midday in Kyoto I only wanted to sleep.

I got undressed in no time and flung myself onto the futon, which no longer seemed so hard. In order to stop thinking about my problems with the wretched postcards, I went back to the first essay I'd read about *wabi-sabi*.

> Everything that exists in the universe is in constant movement and always changing. Nothing is eternal, nothing has existed or will exist for ever, and everything has a beginning and an end. *Wabi-sabi* art can embody or suggest the essential, obvious feature of impermanence and thus lead viewers into a state of serene contemplation which comes with understanding the fleeting nature of everything that exists. Once aware of this transience, we see life from another perspective.
>
> A man may be moved by the sight of a simple flower in an old bamboo vase when he realizes that it reflects life and our destiny as human beings.

Experiencing with Gabriela that "everything has a beginning and an end" had been quite painful, but right then, in that austere room, I was all for transience.

Visit a couple of temples in case anyone asks you about Kyoto and then get a plane home. It has been a mistake to come here, and it would be an even bigger mistake to stay on. Or so I told myself as my eyes were closing.

Only God Knows the Answer

When I opened my eyes again it was after nine at night. I felt my forehead to make sure I wasn't running a temperature. I wasn't in the habit of having afternoon naps lasting more than six hours. And I was cold – too cold.

When I got up, my bones were creaking as if I'd been beaten up. Naked in my spartan room, I dithered over whether I should go down to the *onsen* or have a shower to bring myself back to the waking world. Thinking that the water in the *onsen* would make me even dopier than I already was, I took the latter course.

After dousing myself in lukewarm water, I got dressed: beige cotton trousers and best black T-shirt. I may have looked as if I had somewhere to go to, but the truth was quite the opposite.

As I went down the wooden stairs, I wondered if I was ill. I wasn't hungry, although I'd had nothing to eat since the fish and rice at breakfast.

Was this because of heartbreak? Was I going to waste away like those enamoured young men in romantic novels?

It's pathetic when a man of over forty-five has to suffer like this. I waved at the lady at the reception desk. I'd put the postcards in my pocket – Heaven knows why. The whole thing had turned into a fixation.

Maybe because I'm a creature of habit wherever I am, I took the same route as the one I'd taken the previous night.

The little lantern of the karaoke bar for the lonely gave off its wan glow at the end of the street of geishas. I had no intention of going back there, but as I walked past the door, I saw something that stopped me in my tracks. The iron plaque had been replaced by a wooden one which revealed that, overnight, the place had acquired a name.

SAMUEL'S BAR

Astounded by this, I quickly realized that it must have been that Japanese eccentric who'd suggested this name to the owner.

I pushed open the door. I wanted an explanation for what I thought was a joke in bad taste, and I was sure that the perpetrator would be there in a huddle with his bottle of sake.

Contrary to what I expected, there was no one to be seen in the little bar apart from its owner, who smiled at me conspiratorially. She was perfectly aware of who I was. The least she could do after usurping my name for this dive, I thought, was to offer me a drink.

Since she handed me the drinks list with its clearly marked prices, I quickly twigged that I wasn't going to be let off the outrageous mark-up for my first drink.

I asked for an Asahi and sat in the corner I'd occupied the previous night. Like a nightmare running in a feverish loop, some Russian-sounding notes announced that the insidious 'Dokonoko no Kinoko' was about to begin. The difference was that Okamura's seat was empty. The microphone lay on the bar like a shipwreck in a sea of wood.

I was on the alert in case the lady tried to make me sing. My suspicions were reinforced when she put a piece of paper on the bar. Glancing at it, I could see it had some writing on it, and didn't dare to pick it up in case it was a transliteration of the words of the Japanese song.

It turned out to be a translation into English, written with a scratchy biro in what looked like a girl's handwriting. *Wabi-sabi.*

As the syncopated rhythms invaded the small space, I picked up the bit of paper and started to read.

Hey, mushroom, where are you from?
Beautiful mushroom, where are you from, sir?
A mushroom from the forest.
A forest mushroom turned into a trumpet
And its music flew to the clouds
Puppu-Lu-Papa-Pulu Pappa…
Don't tell this story to the sky.

Hey, mushroom, where are you from?
Beautiful mushroom, where are you from, sir?
A mushroom from the sky.
A sky mushroom turned into a parachute
And fell upon blue waves.
Sulusulu-Lala, Sulu-Lala…
Don't tell this story to the sea.

Hey, mushroom, where are you from?
Beautiful mushroom, where are you from, sir?
A mushroom from the sea.
A sea mushroom turned into a jellyfish
And dreamed of the green forest.
Yurayura-Lu Lu Lu Lu-Yura
Don't tell this story to anyone.

Hey, mushroom, where are you from?
Beautiful mushroom, where are you from, sir?
A mushroom from the forest.
Only God knows the answer.

I hadn't got to the last line of these crazy lyrics when the black door opened and Okamura made a triumphal entrance. He was much more elegant than the previous night and, despite the scratched pebble lenses, I could see from his eyes that he hadn't started drinking yet.

He sat on his stool and, looking at the stranded microphone and addressing it rather than me, announced, "Things will happen today."

I thought that any moment Okamura would ask for a song and grab the microphone, but he didn't. Perhaps he needed the encouragement of a bottle of sake in order to get going.

As he filled his glass with beer, he gazed at me attentively as if he couldn't understand why I'd come back to this place. I certainly knew why I had.

"Can you explain why this bar is now called after me?"

"It is only a name," he replied, unruffled. "Last night, when I was helping the owner with her catalogue of videos, I had the idea we could call it this. She was agreed with me. It is provisional, like life itself. Tomorrow maybe it has another name."

This man was an expert at beating about the bush, even in a language that wasn't his own, so I didn't pursue my unanswered question. After all, he'd simply painted on a wooden board a name that had been given to millions of people around the world.

"How was your day?" I said, changing the subject. "You look very elegant."

"Thank you. I am waiting for my niece. We arranged to have a drink together before she goes to climb mountain for ten days. I do not want Mizuki to see me drunk and take this memory of me to the peak of mountain."

"What mountain is she going to climb? Mount Fuji?"

Okamura took off his glasses, looking very surprised, and peered at me out of eyes that seemed sunk deep in the depths of a valley.

"This is silly. My niece, she is serious climber of mountains. At Mount Fuji there is queue of thousands of people who go from one refuge to next. The path from first to the fifth station has asphalt. I need to say more? From there to tenth refuge is harder. But it is like big department store in sales, except you are very high and you have breathing problem for altitude sickness."

This image of masses of suffocating people bore little resemblance to the pure, sublime view I'd had from the train. No doubt some things are better seen from a distance.

A nostalgic song was now playing in the bar. Okamura half-closed his eyes as if trying to salvage some memory from the past. "The last time I climbed this mountain my wife was ill. She was still enough strong to climb, so we took bus from Kawaguchiko, the nearest town. It left us at fifth station. We needed whole day to get to top, although we both were using two walking sticks because it rises 1,400 metres in only six kilometres."

"What's the peak like?" I suddenly felt a thrill of interest.

"This is a crater full of snow. You can go round it until you reach highest point. There I set my camera on automatic to take last photo of us smiling. When we descended from Mount Fuji, our life also went down."

The wistful song had ended, but the bar owner didn't put on any more music, as if – despite the foreign language we were using – she understood that we were talking about something important.

A tear seemed about to fall from one of Okamura's sunken eyes. "The best thing of life also ends."

"But you're still working." I was trying to shift the conversation into happier terrain. "Do you like your job?"

"It is a business it also is going down. Like me. I am salesman and accountant of a printing company. Now, with digital technology, well, our production it is half, and again half of that. It is miracle we can still pay the paper."

He pronounced the word "paper" like someone mentioning a product from faraway times, like parchment in

Ancient Egypt. That reminded me of the postcards in my trouser pocket.

"Do you know, by any chance," I said, pulling them out, "where this address is?"

Okamura put on his scratched glasses again and held the address with the number 27 close to his face. He looked nervous and shook his head. Then he looked at the stamp with the four women and the telescope and scratched at the edge of the postmark with the nail of his index finger, whereupon the stamp lifted with surprising ease. Then he looked at me accusingly and snapped, "I am old man, but I am not fool. Do you think is amusing to make joke of tired and alone printer?"

"I don't understand what you mean. I don't know what kind of address this is but, if I have offended you, please…"

"There is nothing here that I can read."

"But it's written in kanji…"

"With signs that do not have meaning because the way they are together. The same thing with postmark." He looked daggers at me through his thick lenses.

"They don't mean anything?" I couldn't understand what was going on.

Okamura took a long swig of his beer, trying to calm down. He put the postcard on the bar, looked at me warily and said, "That is not Japanese or any language. Apart from number 27, it is mess of signs written together by one completely ignorant person. It does not make sense whatever."

"But… wait a minute." I took back the postcard with the picture of the cat feeling totally perplexed. "This looks as if it has been printed. How is it possible that…"

"This is made with one person's printer in home," he interrupted. "Someone has made this stupid thing with Photoshop. The stamp they print with postmark. All is false."

I was stunned – so shocked that I didn't notice the door opening to let in a girl who would remain engraved on my memory for ever afterwards.

Postcards That Travelled Down Fourteen Steps

The first thing I thought when I saw Okamura's niece was that she was beauty incarnate. She wasn't wearing a filmy dress and neither was she made up to look like a modern geisha. She must have been about thirty and was wearing jeans, a long-sleeved T-shirt and trainers. Her black hair was simply pulled back in a ponytail – yet she radiated sensuality and elegance.

Mizuki was quite tall, and her face was slightly angular. I guessed she was the daughter of an American father and Japanese mother. Her features were clearly oriental, but her frank gaze was that of a West Coast girl, and there was nothing docile about her.

I forgot about the postcard for a moment and bowed my head at the newcomer, who broke the local rules by holding out her hand for me to shake. It was somewhere between the traditional Japanese greeting and the two kisses we give in the south of Europe.

Once I'd recovered from her appearance, my eyes went back to the postcard. Now I understood everything and I wanted to throttle Titus.

I could imagine him printing the postcards and then using Photoshop to add the meaningless address. He'd even printed and cut out the two stamps with their postmarks.

Humiliated, I now understood why not even the taxi driver wanted to have anything to do with me once I'd shown him the back of the postcard.

Mizuki dragged me out of my peevish musings by asking for cold sake for the three of us. While she filled my ceramic cup, I gave Okamura a short account of how I'd been the victim of a hoax that had dragged me more than ten thousand kilometres away from home.

He was very interested to know more about this man called Titus who wrote books using pseudonyms like Francis Amalfi or Gottfried Kerstin. Watched attentively by his niece, I told him about Titus's work, how he'd started writing a book about *wabi-sabi* and how I was supposed to be helping him with it.

"It's a very poetic way of getting you to make the journey," Mizuki offered. "It must have meant a lot of work for him, printing those postcards so they looked as if they'd come from Japan."

"He wants to write a commercial book about *wabi-sabi*, and that's all there is to it. Since he's old and frail and in no condition to travel, he fooled me into coming here instead."

No sooner were the words out of my mouth than I regretted them. Titus had tried to help me when I most needed him. After my sentimental fiasco, he'd probably got me to fly far away from home to sort myself out. Gabriela would almost certainly know about his plan. Otherwise she wouldn't have written "This person will find you if he wants to" – if her words meant what I thought they did.

Bloody Titus, I've found you out. You're going to pay dearly for this. The postcards which I'd believed were sent from the other side of the world had only needed to go down fourteen steps to find me.

"I'm starving," Mizuki said. "Shall we go and have a barbecue, Uncle?"

Her English was perfect, which reminded me that Okamura had told me that she gave him lessons. As if they were practising conversation, he took care with his pronunciation when answering: "I am not of the mood, my dear. I want to go home now. But the *gaijin* will go with you. OK, Samuel?"

It was impossible to refuse without looking like a complete oaf and, to tell the truth, I wanted to go. Apart from Mizuki's particular brand of hybrid beauty, I was keen to know more about this Japanese woman who moved between two worlds.

"I didn't know you had barbecues in Japan," was my idiotic response, "but I'd be delighted to come with you."

A Circle of Ashes

It was now after eleven and I was following Mizuki through ever-darker alleyways. I say "following" because she was striding along a couple of steps ahead of me, apparently not caring whether I was close behind her or dropping back. As if concentrating hard on finding the way, she hadn't said a word to me since we'd left the bar.

Lagging behind, I could watch her movements in the shadows. Her clothes may have been simple but, with every step, her hips swayed with a hint of sensuality. Even the way her ponytail swung back and forth across her straight back had something of a hypnotic, ancestral dance.

We left the neighbourhood of old houses to walk through a more modern, cluttered part of the city, although the buildings were still low. My guide stopped before a wooden door with a grille through which a pale orangey light shone.

A few seconds after she rang the bell, the door slid sideways, leaving just enough space for one person to squeeze through. On the other side, the silhouette of a very thin man spoke to Mizuki in Japanese.

He finally moved away from the slit in the doorway so that we could enter. It was a tavern-like space, furnished with four barrels with stools around them and lit by a couple of wall lamps. At that time of night, we were the only people there.

The owner pointed with both hands at one of the barrels and disappeared behind a red curtain which, I imagine, was there to separate the kitchen from the customers.

"I think he was about to close and now we've gone and ruined his plans to get some rest," I remarked.

"Fuck him."

"You sound like a rude little brat from Los Angeles," I chided.

"Almost – except I'm from San Francisco and I'm not little. I'll be thirty in a week."

"Happy birthday in advance. Your uncle told me you're going mountain-climbing."

"Sort of. Does throwing yourself into a precipice from a very high mountain come under the heading of mountain-climbing?"

"I think so." I wasn't going to let her wind me up. "At least, people who throw themselves off mountains have to be good climbers."

"Well, that's how I'm going to celebrate the big three. Nobody wants to turn thirty, however much people pretend they do."

The owner-cook-waiter came out with two bowls of miso soup, thus putting an end to this cynical, rather dark conversation. Mizuki asked for two beers and rested her chin on her interlaced fingers. "Tell me about you. Why have you come to Kyoto all by yourself?" Before I could reply, she added, "And don't tell me you're here just because someone put a postcard under your door. You'd have to be a complete idiot!"

I took a mouthful of my Asahi, trying to resist the urge to slap her. Looking at her in the emptiness of the tavern, I suddenly saw her as a poor girl lost between East and West. Since, in all likelihood, this would be the last time we'd meet, I didn't mind opening up.

"Well, I'm helping my old friend Titus by looking for material on *wabi-sabi*. I'm reading about it now and hope to talk to some artists or philosophers who can tell me more."

Just then, the owner appeared with a steaming container and tongs, which he put on one of the stools so he could lift the top of the barrel to reveal a sand-covered base. He then made a circle of glowing coals on the sand and placed the grill on top of them.

"Now he'll bring fresh vegetables and three kinds of meat so we can cook them as we like," Mizuki explained before returning to our conversation. "So… you've come here expressly to learn about the art of imperfection?"

"That's my excuse. I don't want to feel I'm wasting my time here. I'd like to think I'm doing something."

"You're always doing something," she said, gazing into my eyes. "Now you're having a barbecue with me."

Instead of coming out with the riposte that was on the tip of my tongue – *I mean doing something useful* – I adopted a confidential tone – the result of my addled, jet-lagged state and the weird situation of being in this place with a beautiful stranger.

"The truth is I had to get away from Barcelona for a while. The woman I've been with for eight years has left me, and now I'm trying to find my place in the world. You know what I mean?"

"Yes, I know well." Her soft, cold hand covered mine. "I'm in the same situation but in reverse. I've just left the love of my life in San Francisco – now I think I've made a huge mistake."

"It's better to be in your situation than mine. You can always go back to him. I'm sure he's still in love with you."

Mizuki stroked her ear, then said, "I'm still in love with him too, but it's impossible to go back. Things happened and they can't be undone. That's why I want to disappear. For ever."

An expert at dealing with students falling apart because of their difficulties with German, I patted her hand a couple of times.

"Things always happen." Your uncle said so tonight, as soon as he came into the bar."

Mizuki mouthed something inaudibly in Japanese before she switched to English. "There are some things that should never have happened. That's why I left America and have been living with my uncle for the last three months. He's the person I love most in the world, and I wanted to say goodbye to him."

"Say goodbye?"

"Yes, before putting an end to it all." She took a deep breath. "I'm not as great a mountain climber as I've led him to believe. I've never done a solo climb of any mountain of over three thousand metres. I only decided to go to the mountains in Hokkaido because a lot of the land there is uninhabited. I've planned it carefully."

"What have you planned?" I was alarmed.

The cook had placed beside us a tray with different types of meat and a bowl with mushrooms, onion and halved corn cobs.

Without looking up from the circle of coal, which lit up the chalk-white skin of her face, Mizuki continued, "Before my final excursion I'll destroy all my documents and anything that might identify me. Then I'll climb up to the highest peak I can find, sing a song and then jump into the abyss. The End."

"Don't be silly. Let's eat," I said, picking up some bits of meat and vegetables and placing them over the embers.

Mizuki clutched my free hand to make me understand that she was serious. Her tense expression showed suffering and determination.

"My uncle will never know I've died. I'll just be one of those mountain climbers who disappear without trace and nobody ever hears from them again. He will think I have decided to stay on the mountain to live in a little hut, or that I have met a man and run away with him without a word to anyone. That would be very much in character."

"They're all possibilities." I turned the bits of meat over so they wouldn't burn. "But it would be very stupid to kill yourself on your thirtieth birthday. It's in a week's time, right?"

"Yes – it seems a good time to get out of here. What's stupid about that?"

I tried to think while I shifted vegetables around the grill. I didn't want them to get charred. "You can get out whenever you want, but you have to put your affairs in order first. When people love you, you can't just go leaving them in the lurch."

"What do you mean?"

"Your uncle said he's making good progress with his English thanks to you. Learning the language has been keeping him going since he lost his wife," I said. "If you jump off the mountain before you finish your classes, you won't be showing much consideration for your pupil."

That said, I used my chopsticks to pick up a cluster of tiny mushrooms and dip them in the soya sauce. When I tried them they were crisp and tender.

Mizuki bit her bottom lip, apparently deep in thought. You didn't have to be a genius to realize that, however good-looking she was, she was quite unstable.

"OK," she said, "I'll give him a few more classes… but on one condition."

"What condition?"

"You have to promise not to leave until I come back from Hokkaido."

I raised my arm to ask for another beer. I'd fallen into my own trap. She was about to scupper my plan – see a couple of temples and then go home. Then I came to my senses.

"I can't hang around here for ten days waiting for you to come back, Mizuki."

"Ah, no?" She pouted – the perfect brat.

Juggling plans I didn't have, I said, "I can promise to wait if you come back on your birthday. I'll use the week to do some tourism and collect material for my friend."

"Done."

I was surprised that she should agree so readily. Then again, it was simply further proof that she was quite unhinged, showing how her thinking swung wildly from one idea to another. I dipped a bit of meat into the sauce as she gazed at the circle of embers, as if mesmerized by them. She'd hardly even tasted the vegetables.

"Let's do that, then..." I was being very patient. We'll meet at Samuel's Bar next Thursday and celebrate your thirtieth birthday with your uncle. Then we can come back here, if you like."

"I'm only going to do a couple more classes. You need to understand that." Her tone was unexpectedly cold. "I'm like this circle, which will soon turn into ashes. My body's not yet cold, but the fire that used to warm my soul went out a long time ago."

THE SAD SONGS BAR

The Man Alone in Tokyo

I spent the last week of spring getting the most out of my Japan rail pass and hoping to learn something about the country. From Kyoto I went to Nara, which is known for its giant Buddha inside an equally enormous wooden temple. In order to reach the Enlightened One you have to cross a park where deer nip tourists' backsides in the hope they'll drop the biscuits they've brought for them.

My next stop was Osaka – a totally unprepossessing city by day which, at night, turned into a futuristic scene with girls wearing impossible dresses and bizarre makeup parading around under the neon lights.

I spent barely two days in Tokyo, because it was too immense for me. I only had time to go to the fish market, the upscale shopping area of Ginza, the statue of Hachiko – the faithful Akita dog which inspired the film – and the fifty-second floor of the Park Hyatt Hotel.

From this lofty tower, in the New York Bar, famous for appearing in a scene of *Lost in Translation*, I welcomed the start of summer on the Tuesday evening. In memory of the film's languid character, I ordered a Suntory Hibiki 17 whisky and watched night falling over the megalopolis.

Meanwhile, a Diana Krall clone at the piano purred a standard American repertoire which sounded like canned music to my ear.

Perched at the bar next to the window, I alternated between staring out at the vertiginous view of the city and reading my Lonely Planet guide as the Japanese malt scalded my throat.

I calculated that each sip ripped two euros out of my travelling budget.

There's something mystical yet sad about a person going on holiday alone. I'd thought back more than once to some of my weekend trips with Gabriela, when – in London for example – seeing a man dining alone in a Chinese restaurant in Soho, or a foreign girl in Paris wandering all by herself through the Louvre, I wondered whether that solitude was voluntary or imposed by circumstances.

It's not always easy to distinguish one situation from another. Some people leave their partners because they want to be alone and are fed up with the domestic bickering that has become the background noise of everyday life. Others learn the advantages of solitude after being abandoned – and this wasn't my case – and rediscover personal pleasures they've neglected while trying to fit in with someone who, viewed from the perspective of separation, has turned out to be from a very different world.

How much are we able to accept life's changing seasons?

But let's not kid ourselves. Solitude is scary, and very few people would break off a relationship in order to live alone. What people usually do is to change one partner for another who looks like a better alternative.

This wasn't my case, or Gabriela's either, if I was to believe her.

While I was pondering all this, the sunlight slipped away from the host of skyscrapers around me and the neon lights came on.

I couldn't help remembering what an old friend from the faculty once told me: he couldn't imagine greater solitude than that of a man all by himself in Tokyo, surrounded by millions of people and with no one to talk to.

I was that man, all by himself in Tokyo.

Turning into a Flower

On the last day of my mini-tour of Japan I went to Nikko, a mountain town surrounded by shrines and temples, 140 kilometres north of Tokyo.

Despite the short distance involved, getting there in *Shinkansen* land was a minor odyssey. You have to go to the industrial city of Utsunomiya to get the local train, which seems to have had its last refurbishment in the Seventies.

Sitting on a sideways bench upholstered in red velvet, I was prompted by my first sight of woods in the countryside to return to Titus's book. After I left Osaka we'd waged a lengthy WhatsApp war. It had taken him a while to admit he was the author of the postcards that had lured me to the other side of the world, but he'd eventually confessed.

At this distance, I couldn't see his expression, but I thought his remorse was sincere. He even offered to reimburse me for what I'd spent on my flights, paying me in instalments after September. "But I won't cover your accommodation, food and drinks, because you're the one who's sleeping, eating and drinking," he'd said.

I'd replied, "We'll see."

As for Gabriela, we'd exchanged a couple of messages at the most. I asked her if she knew about Titus's hoax and, while acknowledging that she did, added that it hadn't been her idea. She was still in Paris and was showing signs of an oncoming depression.

As if I give a damn, I thought, when I remembered her. The train trundled on, bearing me, in that antiquated carriage, through a dreamscape of bluish hilltops where it had just started to rain.

As if having a *satori*, I suddenly had the insight that this gently undulating countryside was a perfect image of my inner topography. The only good thing about being a middling kind of man is that catastrophes, too, are homely.

I flipped through the anthology, looking for the text about this kind of awakening. The author was D.T. Suzuki, the man who introduced Zen into the West. He says that meditation seeks as its ultimate end the fusion of subject and object, observer and observed. Only when we penetrate the essence of things can we understand them in their profundity – an idea which Suzuki explains beautifully by taking as his example a person absorbed in meditation and a flower:

> To know the flower is to become the flower, to be the flower, to bloom as the flower and to enjoy the sunlight as well as the rainfall. When this is done, the flower speaks to me and I know all its secrets, all its joys, all its sufferings – that is, all its life vibrating within itself. Not only that: along with my "knowledge" of the flower, I know all the secrets of the universe, which includes all the secrets of my own Self, which has been eluding my pursuit all my life so far, because I divided myself into a duality, the pursuer and the pursued, the object and the shadow. […]
>
> Now, however, by knowing the flower I know my Self. That is, by losing myself in the flower, I know myself as well as the flower.

It was a simple but uplifting idea. I had to read the text a couple of times to understand what it was saying. What, then, does the flower teach us? Does it only teach us to look? Maybe when we learn to contemplate the smallest things without filters, we'll be able to turn our eyes towards ourselves.

Very few things are beautiful or ugly. Beauty and ugliness are only in the eye of the beholder.

This thought took me back to Mizuki. It was only five days since I'd been at the bar and the barbecue place with her, but my travelling seemed to have dilated our period of separation.

I imagined her climbing the craggy mountains on the island in the north of Japan. We'd arranged to meet the following night in the bar named after me, but I was suddenly assailed by fear. What if Mizuki had gone through with her original idea and would never come back?

I calmed myself with the thought that the person who really plans to commit suicide never announces the intention but simply goes ahead and does it.

With this foggy, changing mental landscape matching the one all around me, the train stopped in Nikko.

See No Evil, Hear No Evil, Speak No Evil

I woke up in a Nikko guesthouse with five other roommates. The night had brought a relentless concert of snores and sighs, and even a soliloquy in Japanese. Though I'd woken up several times, the fir trees outlined against the moonlight had soothed me. I'd dropped back into an even deeper sleep in the company of their silhouettes, which I could see through the window at the foot of my bed.

I had breakfast feeling as if I'd been resting for days. Perhaps my spirit needed to be surrounded by forests and I'd unjustly confined it to the city.

In the dining room there were three Japanese girls in Boy Scout caps, who got into a huddle and started whispering as soon as they saw me coming down, plus another man of about fifty – bald, moustachioed and dressed in Tyrolean shorts with braces and heavy-duty shoes.

He raised his hand to greet me, and a minute later we were chatting over our fried eggs and beans. There's an unwritten law decreeing that solitary travellers should start to talk and then end up walking together.

He introduced himself as Hans Martin from the Swiss town of Sankt Gallen. After years of wanting to explore Japan, he'd overcome his fear of planes and set out on his solitary adventure. I merely mentioned my *wabi-sabi* story and told him that I was returning to Kyoto that afternoon.

"I think the three wise monkeys would be a major inspiration for your book," he said.

Of course, I knew about this wooden sculpture of a group of monkeys in which one covers its ears with its hands, another covers its mouth and a third covers its eyes, but I didn't know what they were doing in Nikko.

Hans Martin turned out to be an expert on the matter. "They are seventeenth-century carvings mounted over the stables at the Toshogu shrine. It is not far from here. I will accompany you if you like."

"I'd like that very much." I was surprised by his courtesy. "It will be a pleasure and, moreover, I don't have much time for visiting the temples. I have to get on the train after lunch."

"Well, if you can only see one thing, it should be Toshogu."

Not long afterwards, we were on our way, crossing immaculate forests, radiant in the morning light. The strange calm that had pervaded me during the night grew with every step. At that hour, we were the only ones out and about except for the birds trilling in the top branches.

"It must be wonderful to study the beauty of what is imperfect," Hans Martin commented as he guided me along a tree-shaded path. "There are many people trying to make everything smooth and uniform. But the world is wrinkled and cracked. Nothing ever turns out the way it is supposed to – and that is a good thing, because otherwise it would be terribly boring. Do you know what Tagore says?"

"Lots of things, I suppose. Did he talk about *wabi-sabi* too?"

"In his way. He said the forest would be very sad if only the good singers among the birds sang."

Those words made a deep impression on me. As we continued walking in silence, I thought they should apply to love as well. It would be tragic if this was a field reserved only for the most attractive, empathetic and seductive people, because they are precisely the ones who don't need love. They have enough with the admiration they get from everyone around them.

People with broken or yearning hearts are the ones who need to be loved, and if they haven't yet learnt the song of life, they should be able to sing it beside another bird that knows it and will perhaps help them to sing it sweetly.

I was lost in thought when we reached a *torii* at the entrance to the shrine, consisting of two columns topped by an upwardly curving horizontal beam. Hans Martin seemed happy to be at Toshogu, although it was the third time he had been there in the last two days.

"Let us go and see Mizaru, Kikarazu and Iwarazu," he said with boyish enthusiasm.

"Who are they?"

"The three wise monkeys, man! Those are their names, and they mean 'see no evil, hear no evil and speak no evil'."

He led me through small shrines and wooden altars richly adorned with human and animal figures. The likeness of a black-and-white cat sleeping between lotus flowers caught my eye but, without a doubt, the greatest attraction at Toshugo was the *san saru* group.

I stood before the monkeys, which so eloquently expressed their rejection of the three senses.

"Do you know why they're doing that, Hans?"

"There are several interpretations. One is that if you wish to be pure at heart you must never hear, speak or see evil, because it defiles the mind."

"Then we should never turn on the news."

"It depends what the news is."

That rather vague reply put an end to our conversation about the monkeys.

Whither Our Island of Eels?

The trip back to Kyoto took ages, because I had to get the slow train to Utsunomiya and then two bullet trains. It was dark when I arrived.

Although the futuristic architecture of the station surprised me once again, I had the sensation of coming home after my week of travelling. Nikko is a small place surrounded by forests and Tokyo is an endless concrete forest where one can feel equally lost.

Kyoto is the perfect size for a city, I thought as I got into a taxi and set off for the Blue Frogs *ryokan*. Although it was an extravagance, I'd decided to go back there because I liked staying in the same street as the karaoke bar for the lonely.

The tiny receptionist bowed and led me to the same room I'd occupied six nights earlier. Under the lukewarm shower I had the sense that my trip had been only a dream. Everything seemed to be in the same place, and so was I.

This time, however, I had a mission: I'd promised Okamura's niece that we'd meet that evening. I was going to keep my promise, and if she turned up at the karaoke bar, she would be keeping hers too.

At half-past nine I saw that it still bore my name. What had first seemed offensive and then ridiculous now seemed to be a sign that harmony reigned in my little Kyoto universe.

I pushed open the black door and, as if in a new round of an old game, the impassive owner pointed at the stool I'd occupied the first two nights. Once again, I was the only customer, but the music was turned up full blast with a song that was even more raucous and harder on the ear than the mushroom one.

If I'd known a bit more Japanese than a couple of greetings, I would have used it to ask the lady to turn off this annoying music immediately. Instead, I sat there stock-still, watching as she served my Asahi.

The door opened and Okamura came in. This time he was dressed in a pin-striped navy-blue jacket with a sky-blue tie. His grey hair was neat: the first night I saw him he must have been battling the memory of his wife with sake and the microphone.

"*Konbanwa*," I said, then added: "Can you ask her to turn down the volume, please?"

"Why? It is almost finished... You do not like eels?"

"Is it about eels?" I was surprised.

"Yes, it's about eels and hope. This is a very popular song."

I held my tongue. This was really a nation of eccentrics if a song about wild mushrooms and another about eels were in their charts.

The black door opened again. Mizuki had not only safely returned from the mountains, but she was dressed to kill.

The Happiness of the Ainu

I was led along the same route from the old city of Kyoto to the more modern neighbourhood of low houses by a woman I barely recognized. It was as if instead of spending a week in the mountains, Mizuki – now dressed in a black miniskirt, mesh stockings and high heels – had been doing the rounds of the boutiques in Tokyo's trendy nightlife and fashion district of Shibuya.

Once again, I was walking half a metre behind her so I could admire her long legs and the hole in the back of her red top, which revealed black bra straps. This time she didn't have a ponytail, but wore her hair in a plait wound around a high chignon. The Japanese girl from San Francisco had gone from being suicidal to becoming a fashion victim, and I was disconcerted.

On the way to the barbecue place she offered no explanation. She ignored me until we reached the wooden door with the grille. After ringing the bell, she turned around and winked at me.

The skinny man opened the sliding door wide as soon as he saw us. Although we'd come quite a lot earlier this time, we were still his only customers.

We sat down at the same barrel. Apart from the radical change in Mizuki's appearance, I thought everything would be exactly the same as last time. She, however, took it upon herself to prove me wrong.

A large bottle of cold sake landed on top of the barrel just as she was saying: "Now we have to celebrate the fact that we've both come back."

"Did you doubt it?"

"I knew you'd be here," she said, staring at me with a strange, fixed expression on her face. "I wasn't so sure about myself."

I drank half a glass of the unfiltered sake, while analysing her first statement. Her conviction that I would be there meant that she was very well aware of how attractive she was, or she had detected in me a fearful soul that didn't want to feel guilty about a suicide.

From my side of the barrel I watched the light of the lantern shine playfully over her face. My gaze dropped for a moment below her shoulders.

"Tell me what you did in Hokkaido." I said, recovering my composure. "Is it true that the monkeys there bathe in the hot springs?"

"You mean the macaques? If you want to see them in the hot springs, you have to go there in winter, when the temperatures drop to fifteen below zero. But not in Hokkaido. They are in the mountains of Nagano. I spent the whole week with an indigenous community. The Ainu," she added, sniffing her glass of sake.

"Ainu," I repeated. "I've never heard of them. In fact, I didn't even know that Japan had indigenous people."

"There are only a few thousand now. They're animists and believe that everything on earth has its *kamui*, or divine spirit. They bless the spirits of wine and food before they eat and drink, and live in thatched houses they call *cise*."

"Apart from that, are they like other Japanese? Do the girls dress… like you?"

"No way!" Mizuki looked at me as if I was teasing her. "I've dressed up like this because I've spent too many days sleeping on the floor in a reed hut like any other Ainu. I'm telling you, they're different from us in everything. For example, they don't have furniture."

Two bowls of miso soup arrived as Mizuki's mood became more expansive. She was fascinated by what she'd seen.

"The men have very long beards and moustaches, and the women tattoo a wide black smile on their mouths and also their genitals. They're all loaded with earrings and other trinkets. They hunt whatever they can find in the forest using a bow and poisoned arrows." She blew on her soup before concluding. "The men only use chopsticks when they're eating to move their moustaches out of the way. The women use spoons."

"I'm happy that you've come back in better spirits," I said, before starting on my soup. "Did the Ainu teach you their language?"

"It's very difficult and nothing like Japanese. I only learnt one word, *anekuroro*. It means 'happy'. The old lady in my hut said it every time I thanked her for the good food."

"*Anekuroro*... I don't know how long I'll be in Kyoto, but I'm happy to see you happy."

Mizuki slowly savoured her soup, her eyelids lowered but looking relaxed. Then she smiled and said something I didn't understand.

"Tonight you'll have the chance to prove that what you just said is true."

Namida No Cafe

After dinner Mizuki took me to the crowded Shijō-dōri Avenue in the centre of town, running from the Yasaka shrine to a bustling area around the Shijō Bridge, which crosses the Kamo River.

As we made our way through a traffic jam, amid the hum of music from the *pachinko* parlours, I was surprised by the architectural chaos. Avant-garde buildings of three or four storeys rose next to insipid little poster-covered cubicles and luxury office blocks. Looking at the tangled messes of electrical cables connecting these buildings, I thought that one spark could plunge the whole city into darkness.

"It's down here," Mizuki said, taking my hand and pulling me into an alley that branched off the main road. "Now you're going to discover my favourite bar."

As we ventured deeper into the narrow, almost dark street, I was shocked by how cold her skin was. It was as if I was being guided by a beautiful reptile. On several floors of buildings that looked only half finished, scattered light bulbs lit up posters in kanji announcing a variety of businesses.

"Are they brothels?"

"Some of them must be, but it's very usual in Japan to have shops on any floor of a building. We have such a big population that there isn't room for all the businesses on the ground floor."

We stopped outside a small building covered in white tiles, which reminded me of the first apartment blocks to be constructed on the Costa Brava. The outside stairway went up past four bars with hand-painted signs on wooden plaques. The one at attic level showed an alien's head with a tear on its cheek.

"It's the bar at the top," she said, ahead of me on the stairs.

On the way up to Namida no Cafe – whose name, as the sign suggested, meant Bar of Tears – I looked into bar rooms as tiny as the one where we'd met, although they were much more stylish. There was one named Yellow which, honouring its name, was totally painted in that colour, from floor to walls and furniture. Even the waiter's shirt was yellow. Mizuki's favourite bar turned out to be a shadowy place of some fifteen square metres with three tiny tables and a sofa. Behind a well-stocked bar a young man sporting a discrete quiff welcomed us with a nod.

He had a tear tattooed beneath his right eye.

A portable record player at one end of the bar supplied the background music. As the record played, I looked at the cover, supported upright by two bottles. Joy Division's 'Atmosphere' was suitably sad.

Mizuki got comfortable on the sofa. I looked around for a stool so I could sit facing her from the other side of a table with a cracked glass top.

"Don't be such a gentleman," she protested. "You can sit next to me."

Trying not to look like a coward, I did what she said, leaving a few inches between us. Meanwhile, she rapidly ordered something in Japanese.

"What did you ask for?" I was edgy.

"Two Stigmata Martyr cocktails. I won't tell you what's in them. Let's see if you can guess."

"The record had stopped spinning, and silence reigned as the barman fixed our drinks.

"This isn't a very cheerful place."

"No, it isn't. After all, it's called 'The Bar of Tears'."

"So have we come here to cry?"

Her tense expression showed that my teasing didn't go down well.

Invasion of Happiness

Two cocktails as red as Mizuki's T-shirt were plonked on the table just as someone else came in. A hairy guy with a strangely long face took his place at the farthest table from us, which was only two and a half metres away.

The boy with the quiff turned on a flat screen inset beneath the bar. It was connected to a YouTube channel with a name that couldn't have been more appropriate: Sad Songs Channel.

'Lost Song' by Ólafur Arnalds, a neoclassical piece for a weepy violin and repetitive, depressing piano came with the image of a frozen flower.

I took a sip of my cocktail, which turned out to consist of tomato juice and gin, and then said to Mizuki, "I'm not surprised that you want to find a precipice and jump to your death if you come to this place often. How come you like it?"

"Namida no Cafe consoles me."

I took a sip of my Stigmata Martyr as I waited for Mizuki to elaborate.

Curled up on the sofa, her expression was one of existential weariness.

"When you're not going through the best time of your life, there's nothing more offensive than an invasion of happiness, when all you want to do is cry. You go into a department store and they put on jolly canned music for shoppers who are laughing and shouting like lunatics. Even in the bar where my uncle goes..."

"Whatever you say, that song about the eels is terrible."

"There are some that are much worse than that, believe me." A faint smile flickered across her face. "What I like about this place is that you don't have to pretend to be happy or cover your ears, or hate anyone. The songs are in tune with my spirit which, basically, is at rock bottom. Here, I feel as if things are the way they ought to be."

"The mood of our spirit changes like the seasons of the year. Not even sunny days or extreme cold last for ever, but I understand that it's difficult to see that when you're really down in the dumps."

She gave me a bored look. I could see that my words were water off a duck's back, so I tried a different tack, hoping to find out why she was so unhappy.

"What was your husband like?"

Mizuki shook her head slowly, as if waking up from a dream.

"Richard was a good man, maybe even too good. He was so true to his principles that I could always work out what he was going to do next. He became totally predictable."

"So did you leave him because of that?" I was looking for some connection with my own case. "Were you bored?"

"It's much more complicated than that… Let's say he was so kind, attentive and understanding that he pushed me into being the opposite. It was sort of like yin and yang. I ended up being his antithesis."

"I don't understand."

"Neither do I." She sighed. "That's why I came back to Japan. I hope the distance will help me figure it out."

We lapsed into silence, but it wasn't uncomfortable. Somehow we'd gone about this backwards. I knew the conclusion of the story, but not the story itself.

Then again, she knew nothing about my little drama, except that I'd been dumped by my partner.

Maybe there was no need to go into details. Perhaps it was enough to know that we'd both failed in love and had ended up in this Bar of Tears, although I no longer had any desire to cry.

As if she'd guessed what I was thinking, Mizuki suddenly said, "I've had enough of this bar for today. Do you want to come to my place?"

"That wouldn't be right." I said. "Don't you live at your uncle's house?"

"I do, but he lives downstairs and I live upstairs. We have separate entrances. What are you frightened of?"

Geikos, *Maikos* and *Dannas*

Without knowing exactly how it happened, I was sitting in a taxi next to Mizuki. I was a cocktail shaker of ominous sensations and desires more difficult to separate than the ingredients in the Stigmata Martyr I'd just had.

As the taxi climbed to an outlying neighbourhood in the foothills of one of the mountains surrounding Kyoto, I glanced at this woman who was pulling me into her private abyss.

Any man in my situation would have tried to spend an unforgettable night with her but, for better or worse, I was full of inhibitions. I went through all of them as the taxi left the city centre behind and entered the residential neighbourhoods.

If she was still married, that was sufficient reason to get no closer than I'd already got. I could put myself in the place of her abandoned husband. Even if she'd come back to Kyoto, I would have been deeply wounded to discover she'd gone to bed with a foreigner she'd just met.

Then there was the question of whether I was free to do what I wanted. Gabriela had asked for a break, but without specifying how long a break. Did that mean I had to wait and be faithful to her in the meantime? Was she still with me, in Paris or wherever she was? Or had she lied when she'd said there was no other man?

Wrapped up in these musings, which only made me feel bad, I felt Mizuki's cold fingers caressing the side of my neck.

"I can see you're tense," she whispered in my ear. "You should relax. I don't have any expectations about what might happen between you and me, if that's what you want to know. I'm living for the moment. When we were in Namida no Cafe, I just wanted to be somewhere quieter with you. That's all."

"I'm flattered," I said, trying to hide my nervousness. "This trip has been revealing. I'm beginning to see that I'm a man who doesn't know how to enjoy the pleasures of life. That's why my partner left me, and that's why you're going to be disappointed at the end of the night."

In response, Mizuki raised her index finger to her nose and smiled. Then she pointed at a small house next to some traffic lights where we'd stopped.

I was amazed to see a geisha coming out carrying something that looked like a lute and then getting into a car with tinted windows. Her movements were so graceful she hardly seemed to touch the ground.

"That's the second one I've seen since arriving in Kyoto."

"You've been lucky then. You don't often see them, especially at night."

"Really? I thought they'd be working at private functions at night."

"They do, but they move around with the utmost discretion, as you've just seen. They very rarely work so late at night, like the one we've just seen." She gave me a provocative look. "Unless they're modern geishas like me."

"Do you see them more often in the morning?"

"Yes. Although there are only about a thousand in Japan now, you can see them early in the morning in Gion, doing errands with their *maikos*."

"What are *maikos*?"

"Apprentice geishas. In Tokyo they start when they're eighteen, but here fifteen is seen as old enough to start learning the arts of the *geiko*, which is what geishas are called here."

"*Geikos* and *maikos*... And what else do they do, apart from playing the lute, getting around with incredible hairdos and performing traditional Japanese arts?"

"Are you insinuating that our *geikos* are prostitutes?"

"Please..." I threw up my arms to protest my innocence. "Nothing was further from my..."

"Even though they flirt in accordance with the old rules and joke with men, their profession always precludes any kind of sexual relationship. What they do traditionally have is a *danna* – a lover-protector who pays for their very expensive training and the other expenses incurred in becoming a geisha."

Just then, the taxi pulled up in front of a two-storey house. Taking the keys from her bag as the car drove off, Mizuki announced, "Now you're going to find out what a modern *geiko* does."

In Praise of Shadows

As Mizuki had said, she had a separate entrance to her apartment. We went up to the second floor by way of a stairway next to the carport. I imagined that Mr Okamura was downstairs sleeping off that evening's bender – it was after two a.m. – while his niece was busy robbing a poor *gaijin* of his peace of mind.

Once again I followed her to a door, with a foreboding that my willpower wouldn't last much longer.

She invited me into her loft, for that's what it was – a clear space with no partitions except for a wide paper screen separating the futon from the rest of the space.

Gentle indirect light radiating from floor level at different points in the room made the place look like a contemporary dance studio.

"This used to be my uncle's atelier," Mizuki told me, "but since my aunt died he's stopped sculpting and works only as many hours as he has to. He spends the rest of his time in that bar in Gion. I think he's got something going with the owner. If not, I don't know why he's always hanging out there."

"Maybe he just wants to sing a song from time to time."

I couldn't imagine any kind of romance with that dry, unfriendly woman. Indeed, I'd never seen them having a single conversation while I was there.

"When I arrived here three months ago, I moved stuff up from the cellar to make my apartment the way I wanted it."

"It's very nice." I took a step towards the screen, imagining that she had a sitting room on the other side.

"No, sit on my bed," she ordered. "Get comfortable. I'm desperate for a shower."

Before I could protest, she disappeared behind the paper partition.

I was totally uncomfortable in this situation, but good manners prevented me from moving to the other part of the loft, where I hadn't been invited. Mizuki might have undressed by now – I'd heard her dropping her shoes onto the wooden floor – and could be walking naked between that part of the flat and the bathroom.

My prim and proper mind only admitted two options: leave immediately and wander round the area looking for a taxi, or do what she'd asked.

I took the latter option, though I couldn't imagine how things would turn out if they continued along the way they now seemed to be going.

Exasperated with myself and my hang-ups, I sat on one side of the bed without even taking off my shoes, facing the screen or room divider – whatever it was – through which one bright light filtered from the other side.

My eyes wandered to the only piece of furniture I could see: a bedside table with a CD player and a book on it. Always curious about books, I couldn't resist picking it up.

It was the American edition of a classic that I'd wanted for ages – Tanizaki's *In Praise of Shadows*, which was published in 1933.

I'd read somewhere that Japanese aesthetics, besides dwelling on imperfection, the organic and the ephemeral, sees shadows as a basic element in the architecture of places.

While in the West we prize what is bright, polished and symmetrical, the Japanese are fascinated by everything that is asymmetrical and veiled in shadows.

I heard the shower being turned on somewhere on the other side of the loft. Befuddled by alcohol and the late hour, and further thrown off-balance by my pleasure on finding that book, my mind wandered to the body that just then was being caressed by warm water.

With butterflies in my stomach, I concentrated on Tanizaki.

What Little Life Remains

I was seduced by Tanizaki's thoughts on the beauty of metals darkened by time. Japan's much-revered novelist was surprised by the fact that westerners set their tables with shiny cutlery. The Japanese consider that such glossiness is very bad taste. When it comes to using kettles, or silver goblets and flasks, they prefer a time-dulled surface, showing that the object has lived and has a story to tell.

Someone once said that a teapot has delicate feelings, because of the people and conversations that have surrounded it. And there was I, discovering the beauty of time-worn things.

Was my soul more beautiful now that it was tarnished after I had been jilted by Gabriela? The extraordinary situation I was in: sitting on the bed of a modern geisha – or *geiko* – might suggest it was.

Of course time takes the shine off everything, but I'd never stopped to think that this dulling of lustre could be seen as beauty. Then I was reminded of something I'd heard about the CVs of some Americans aspiring to an executive position. In Europe people only cite their achievements, but if an American economist goes broke when setting up a business, he includes it among his feats.

What for some people is an embarrassment, for others is an experience that is more valuable than any degree or successful undertaking. A person who has been at the bottom of the well once will take care not to fall in again.

The shower had been turned off, and I was a bundle of nerves. Sitting on the edge of the bed, I hunched over the book like a monk trying to ward off the world's temptations.

> [...] our ancestors, forced to live in dark rooms, presently came to discover beauty in shadows, ultimately to guide shadows towards beauty's ends.
>
> And so it has come to be that the beauty of a Japanese room depends on a variation of shadows: heavy shadows against light shadows – it has nothing else. Westerners are amazed at the simplicity of Japanese rooms, perceiving in them no more than ashen walls bereft of ornament. Their reaction is understandable, but it betrays a failure to comprehend the mystery of shadows.

Tanizaki then explains that indirect lighting is essential for creating beauty inside a Japanese home. The walls are expressly painted in pale, neutral colours to embrace what he calls "faint, frail light".

A fragment from *In Praise of Shadows* made me forget my apprehension for a moment.

> We delight in the mere sight of the delicate glow of fading rays clinging to the surface of a dusky wall, there to live out what little life remains to them. We never tire of the sight, for to us this pale glow and these dim shadows far surpass any ornament.

All at once I realized that it was no accident that I had found this book. It had been placed there deliberately and it was understood that I would read it before experiencing what was about to happen.

Through the paper screen I saw the silhouette of Mizuki dressed in a kimono. The shadow was clear enough for me to see that she'd let down her hair, which now cascaded down her back.

"Could you put on the first track of the CD?" she asked from the other side.

My body was totally tense, but I managed to lift the cover of the CD player to check that there was a CD inside. There was. It was Ryuichi Sakamoto's *BTTB*, and the track she wanted was called 'Energy Flow'.

When the music began, the tenuous light on my side went out, and there was no silhouette on the other side for the light there to outline.

What I saw next took my breath away.

The Shadow Dance

A motionless silhouette stood there facing me and then slowly turned, arms stretched out before it. Dancing to the gentle rhythms of 'Energy Flow', Mizuki, now stripped of her kimono, revealed her naked form.

The shadow dancer raised her arms and tipped her head back to gaze at the ceiling. A long, fine cascade of hair fell on the screen, parallel to her back.

The figure raised one leg and held it in the air, then slowly turned her body, casting pale shadows all around.

Enthralled by the spectacle, all my senses surrendered to the modern *geiko*'s shadow dance. I now understood what Stendhal's syndrome was all about.

When the track finished, the lights in the loft went out.

I remained where I was, sitting on the bed without a clue about what was going to happen next.

I heard the dancer's barefoot steps coming towards me very slowly. Since I couldn't see her, I was surprised to hear a whisper in my ear.

"Do you want me to call a taxi? You must be very tired."

I accepted gratefully, although part of me didn't want to leave that shadow which would very soon turn into a body.

The soft lights on our side of the loft came on. Mizuki, now calling the taxi on her mobile, was wearing her kimono again.

I remembered her words at the barbecue place, before we'd gone to the Sad Songs Bar. She'd claimed that tonight I'd be able to show her that I was happy because she was happy. What did she mean? That the culmination of her desire was that shadow dance?

Surprising me again, Mizuki slipped between the sheets and took off her kimono. With her face sunk into the pillow and her eyes closed, she said, "Watch the screen on my mobile. When it lights up and vibrates twice the taxi will be at the door. Will you turn out the lights with the switch next to the door?"

Half a minute later, her breathing was deep and even. She'd fallen into a peaceful sleep.

I sat in silence beside her. In her slumbers, she didn't care whether I was there or not. Her black hair spread over the pillow – a strange creature with a thousand silken tentacles.

I took a strand and gently ran two fingers along it to feel its texture. It was even finer and more delightful to touch than it looked. I wondered if her skin still felt cold.

The phone on her bedside table lit up and vibrated twice.

It was lucky that the taxi had arrived in time to put an end to these thoughts. I'd seen a naked shadow dancing and had been allowed to watch a *geiko* sleeping. Those two intimate gifts would be enough to nourish my imagination for the rest of my life.

Thinking about it, I needed no more than that.

I drew the sheet over her uncovered arm, turned out the light and went downstairs.

The taxi driver was waiting at the gate with the light inside the car turned on. He was calmly reading a book. As I approached, I felt deep admiration for Japan's silently elegant people.

Existential Angst

After a night of fretful dreams in which Mizuki appeared in turns as an ill-mannered, suicide-prone girl staying with an Ainu group, a *femme fatale* and a dancing shadow, I got out of bed with a bad migraine.

I picked at some fish and rice for breakfast, after which I went to the *onsen* with one of Titus's books. Tipping a bucket of water over my head, I told myself that he would be very disappointed to learn that I hadn't managed to find any new material for his study.

I'd been in Japan for ten days and had made no progress with the subject of *wabi-sabi*, apart from my visit to the three wise monkeys and reading Tanizaki. I didn't even know why my *ryokan* was called Blue Frogs. Where on earth were those impossible frogs?

I immersed myself in the water, puffing like a sumo wrestler. When I sat down on the underwater ledge, the pain began to spread from my head to the rest of my body.

Alone in the *onsen* at that late hour of the morning, I imagined that the other guests in the *ryokan* must be busy doing deals or leaving offerings in one of the city's one thousand six hundred temples. I hadn't seen a single temple yet – which, combined with the little research I'd done, made me feel totally useless.

The best thing I could do would be to return to Barcelona as soon as possible. I could help Titus write the book and prepare my courses for the coming academic year.

When I thought about going back to my old routine, I was swamped by a feeling of bitterness. In Kyoto, at least, I was having strange, dizzying adventures. To begin with, I'd discovered a karaoke bar for the lonely and had spent that incredible evening with Mizuki.

Nevertheless, I knew that, like Gabriela's sojourn in Paris, this was just a detour from my everyday life. I would have to leave soon – partly because I'd almost reached my credit-card limit. In four days' time my Japan rail pass would expire. If I didn't want to pay a fortune to travel to Narita on the bullet train, I'd have to get back to the airport before then.

Caught up in this jumble of practical and existential thoughts, I picked up the *wabi-sabi* anthology.

I found no comfort there. It only made me see that other people much less fortunate than myself were able to enjoy things that I, a completely free man, was denying myself.

How often had I spent a day in the open air these last years? My peaceful walk in Nikko had been my first contact with the countryside in ages. And this is not to mention the other pleasures of life which kept confronting me with the moral dilemmas of a man who keeps hurting himself in order to keep moaning.

Wasn't I a bachelor whose only responsibility was to have the best time I possibly could in one of the world's loveliest cities? So what was the problem?

I didn't know about the frogs, but I did know the answer to this question. I was the problem.

The Temple of the Dragon at Peace

I got dressed and went downstairs. I was astonished to see Mizuki there, sitting in a chair next to the counter. She was now wearing a pretty floral dress and high-heeled shoes, which gave her a romantic, slightly Victorian look. Her hat and sunglasses suggested it was a nice day.

I kissed her on each cheek, just as I would if meeting a Mediterranean girl.

"I thought you only went out at night," I joked. "Though you did tell me that geishas do their errands in the morning. Where do you want me to go with you today?"

"I want to show you something that will give you inspiration for your book. It's not one of the most spectacular temples, but it is the most mysterious."

She held out her hand, a most unusual gesture for a Japanese girl, and we left the *ryokan* together. In Japan couples never walk hand in hand or make displays of affection. But we weren't a couple either. We weren't even friends. What were we then? An intersection between two separate solitudes?

As we walked towards the nearest main road, I asked: "Do you feel more American or Japanese?"

"Culturally I'm Californian. I was ten when my parents moved there for professional reasons." She paused for a moment, then added, "I've spent two thirds of my life in America, so I suppose I'm from there. But, spiritually, I feel Japanese."

A taxi stopped before I could ask what she meant. After some rapid instructions to the driver, she got in and sat resting her hands on her knees.

The taxi made its way through Friday lunchtime traffic. I had no idea where we were going, but I wanted to know more about Mizuki, so I asked her to tell me about her life in California.

"I studied Psychology at Berkeley, but I've never worked as a psychologist. I like art, like my uncle, so I married a man with an open-air gallery near Palo Alto. I ran the business."

"Richard."

"We started living together when I finished my master's. I was twenty-five then. Five years, and we never had a single argument."

Her voice wobbled slightly, but I couldn't see the expression in her eyes behind the dark glasses.

"But if he was a good man and he loved you and you could do the kind of work you enjoyed, why did you leave him?"

"I don't know."

This laconic answer meant she didn't want to talk about it, but I wasn't about to give up now I'd got that far.

"The night we met, you told me you'd made the biggest mistake of your life. You said you're still in love with Richard but now it's impossible to go back. What did you mean?"

Mizuki's face tensed.

"I slept with his best friend. Is your curiosity satisfied now?"

"I'm sorry, I didn't want…"

"The guy had been desperate to get in bed with me for ages, and when it happened he made sure everybody knew about it, including Richard." Her tone was harsh. "He was a total idiot: he thought he could get me that way. But he was wrong. It was all a terrible mess. Then I came to Kyoto. There's no going back."

The taxi drew up at the gates of the Ryōan-ji temple – whose name, according to my guide, meant "Temple of the Dragon at Peace".

Knowing that I'd upset Mizuki, I tried to smooth things over with a typical *gaijin* comment.

"Isn't this is the Zen temple with a very famous dry-landscape garden?"

"It's probably the most famous *kare-sansui* garden in Japan. All Zen followers come to see it, but I doubt you'll understand why."

Dry Landscape

Just as Mizuki had suggested, I failed to see the magic in that expanse of pebbles dotted with rocks. The Japanese visitors, however, stared at it in fascination or kept walking around, looking and taking photos.

When we went to sit on a step facing the garden, Mizuki explained: "The garden consists of fifteen different-sized rocks. It has an odd feature, and that is that wherever you walk, you can only see fourteen rocks, no more, no less."

"So that's the attraction?"

"It's not an attraction. It's a quality," she said. "Imagine, this Zen work has existed since the fifteenth century. It was created by a monk of the Rinzai School."

"So, what does it mean?" I was getting interested. "I suppose the rock islands are not there by chance. They must have some meaning in Zen philosophy."

"Yes, they must have some meaning, but nobody knows what it is. The person who made the garden never left any explanation. That's why it's a mystery, almost like a *koan* – you know, the riddles the old Zen masters asked to cause great doubt and stimulate lateral thinking in their students – but it has no answer."

"It reminds me of the mystery of the *ryokan* where you came to get me. It's called Blue Frogs *ryokan*, but I haven't seen any blue frogs anywhere."

Mizuki took off her glasses and glared at me. My banal comment – fruit of a brain as dry as that garden – had debased a very sacred matter.

We spent the rest of the afternoon visiting two more shrines, one of which was the Kiyomizudera Buddhist temple, made of red wood and surrounded by magnificent forests climbing up the mountainside. Observing tradition, we drank water from one of three channels running down the mountain to a pond.

More than the constructions, what impressed me were the marvellous view of forests on the mountain and the panoramic vistas of Kyoto on the other side. From this height, it looked like a small, modern, soulless city.

Our last stop, just before sunset, was the shrine of Fushimi Inari Taisha – a large complex of Shintu temples, located quite a long way from the city. A group of fox-headed wooden figures in front of the sacred buildings guard the spirits. I was intrigued because they wore bibs with something written on them in calligraphy. But the most impressive sight on that walk were all the incredibly long *torii* paths – red arcades made up of thousands of pillars going all the way up to the top of the mountain.

As we went back to the railway station, I felt so tired I was almost buckling at the knees. Mizuki, on the other hand, was in fine form, like a night bird becoming alert after dark.

"If you come to the bar with me, Samuel, I'll sing you something you'll never forget."

"I was about to say I need to call it a day, but I'd hate to miss the show. What's the song called?"

"'I Look Up when I Walk.'"

After so much trekking from temple to temple, I thought she was just teasing me, but she insisted, saying that it was one of the most famous Japanese songs of all time.

"Is it the one you were thinking of singing before jumping off the mountain?"

"Yes. The title's very appropriate, isn't it?" It was as if she thought suicide was a joke. "But it's not only about climbing mountains or walking along paths. It's a song about happiness and sadness."

Later, on the train taking us back to the city centre, I said, "All right, I'll come with you and hear this song. But I want to know what the words are."

"Don't worry. You'll find out. Meanwhile, I'll sing it for you tonight."

Holes in Your Socks

On the way back to the old alleyway leading to the Blue Frogs *ryokan* and the karaoke bar, Mizuki suddenly said, "Do you know when a couple's love ends?"

I was taken aback by this odd question. "I don't know... When you have an affair?"

"That's a consequence of the end of a relationship, but there are things that indicate it was over a long time before that."

"What things?" This subject was making me feel uncomfortable. "Sorry, perhaps I'm a bit thick and don't see these things. If I'd known..."

"...You wouldn't have let the bird of paradise escape from its cage," she interrupted. "People don't think about what I'm going to tell you now, but it's a very precise description of a relationship. Let's see if I can make it clear..."

We'd reached the bar that bore my name, but didn't go straight in. Leaning against the wall, Mizuki flexed one of her legs while she explained her theory.

"Love is madness and inspiration. Plato said that anyone who's in love becomes a poet. To a greater or lesser extent, people indulge in all kinds of silliness trying to impress the person they love. So, when everything's going well, your partner will surprise you on your birthday or at Christmas with a trip to some place you never dreamt existed, or take you to a special secret restaurant. Things like that." Mizuki paused to take in a deep breath. "So, when couples start giving each other practical gifts, it means their passion has died."

"What sort of practical gifts?" I was getting defensive. My last gift to Gabriela had been to enrol her in a course of Hebrew, which I knew would make her very happy.

"I mean the everyday things you need, useful gifts: an anorak for rainy days, new shoes that look like the scruffy old ones you still keep wearing, T-shirts and underpants. Well, that's if we're talking about clothes. To sum up, they're things you need, but you'd buy them yourself in normal circumstances. Can you imagine Juliet giving Romeo a couple of T-shirts and underpants?"

"I don't like it when you're so cynical." I was getting annoyed. "Maybe it's more romantic to give a hundred roses or a heart made of your own hair, but practical gifts show you don't want your partner to lack anything he needs. If your man has holes in his socks, you give him four new pairs. It's as simple as that. So what's the problem?"

"The problem is that there was a time when your partner used to plan your gift for days, but now it takes him only half a minute to think about it."

"There was a time..." I wanted to rebut this immature idea of love. "There was a time when you didn't even know your beloved had holes in his socks. That kind of knowledge comes with living together, and it's natural that a relationship should move on to more run-of-the-mill things."

As a man who'd been left by his partner without ever having lived with her, I could see that my little speech wasn't very convincing. But I was defending millions of people who turn new underpants, T-shirts and socks into an act of love.

Just then the bar door opened and out came Okamura. It was clear from the way he was shouting that he was drunk again.

"What the hell you are doing out here? This poor old printer does not want to drink by himself."

"Come on, let's go in," I said, happy to be able to change the subject. "Anyway, you owe me a song."

"I plan to be paid for it."

Puzzled by those words, I followed them inside the tiny karaoke bar. Mizuki ordered cold, unfiltered sake for two and then asked the lady to put on 'I Look Up when I Walk'.

From the opening notes of violins and a xylophone, the song sounded as if it was from the year dot. The melody was naively cheerful.

Ue wo muite arukou
Namida ga koborenai you ni
Omoidasu haru no hi
Hitoribotchi no yoru.

Mizuki's voice was sweet and delicate, giving the song a feel of cartoon films from a long time ago.

That was only the first of the songs she and her uncle sang that night, while bottles of sake kept emptying so fast that even the lady behind the bar looked pleased for once.

Give the Idiot a Night of Pleasure

When we left the bar at three in the morning, walking was a major problem. Perhaps because I'd never had a bunch of friends to fool around with, I couldn't remember ever being so drunk.

"You should drink sake more often," Mizuki laughed, slipping her arm round my waist. "Tonight you took off your disguise of the boring professor who's pissed off with the world."

"I don't know who I am tonight."

"So much the better. It's good to get carried away sometimes. How do you want to end the night?"

Earlier we'd been arguing about T-shirts and socks at the door of the bar, and now we were talking at the door of my *ryokan*. I said, "Imagine you're the scriptwriter and director of a film and the male lead is just like me."

She found this amusing. She was smiling and her hair was tousled.

"It's nice of you to give me the job. Tell me more about the film."

"The man in your story is very square and always afraid of making mistakes. He's used to doing the right thing. When it comes to love too."

"Keep going."

"Without really knowing why, this man ends up in Japan. His girlfriend has told him she wants to take a break and he's hardly heard anything from her since then. But being so far from home immediately makes him feel better."

"You mean his girlfriend is fucking someone else but hasn't dared to tell him yet. And then?"

In normal circumstances this comment would have been deeply wounding, but I was too stupefied by liquor to feel pain.

"In his travels, this boring man meets a beautiful, eccentric Japanese woman who was raised in the United States. She's probably the most attractive woman he's ever met in his life, and he even starts dreaming that he might have a chance with her."

"Life throws up many chances." She hiccupped. "Someone said that once."

"Imagine that this chance is within his reach and he desperately wants to make love to her, but he's still dithering."

"What about?"

"This woman has given him a shadow dance, something which he'll never forget, and maybe the film would have a more poetic ending if he leaves it at that and takes this memory home with him instead of consummating his desire. Naturally, this leading man is an idiot."

"You've lost me. What's the question then?"

"If you were the scriptwriter and director, which of the two endings would you choose for him?"

"That's easy. I'd give the idiot a night of pleasure."

Happiness Lies beyond the Clouds

I can remember very little about what happened on the futon – and even then I have to make an effort. Maybe this is a pity. The only time in your life you go to bed with a modern geisha you'd surely want to remember every moment and every inch of her body. But if life's imperfect, your memory of life is even more so.

My first recollection is that of going up to my room in the *ryokan* after the receptionist had implored us not to make any noise as everyone was asleep. Once inside, Mizuki let her floral dress drop to the floor and, wearing only orange lingerie, lay down on the futon.

That was a very unusual colour for underclothes, and the exact shade has remained engraved on my mind. I'd stripped down to my underpants by then, and we lay there talking for quite a while about things I no longer remember.

A second fragment I've retained is the moment when I felt her tongue on mine as I struggled to undo her bra. I've always been clumsy in these matters. That memory ends with the moment when I felt her breasts against my skin as her hand pushed its way into my underpants.

The third scrap consists of a close-up of her face on the pillow, just as I entered her the first time. Her expression was not yet one of pleasure. It was more like – surprise, or even shock, as if to say, *How on earth did this happen*?

Marshalling those fragmentary memories, now with broad daylight shining down on the bed, I got aroused again. But Mizuki wasn't lying there next to me.

When I stood up, I discovered to my relief that I didn't feel too bad. I was slightly woozy, but that was all. Maybe Brian Ferry was right when he said that love is the drug for him.

Breakfast time was long over, so I went directly down to the *onsen*. After the ritual with the bucket of cold water, I took up an underwater seat next to a fat man who wanted to practise his rudimentary English. After asking me where I was from, he came out with the classic question: "Business or pleasure?"

"Pleasure." I was surprised to hear myself pronouncing the word.

Later, when I was about to go out, the tiny woman at the reception desk greeted me with a bow and held out an envelope for me. I carefully opened it and pulled out two sheets of beautiful writing paper folded into quarters. The first sheet was a letter.

Dear Samuel,

Thank you for these fantastic days and nights I've spent with you and, in particular, for waiting for me and giving me strength when I thought I'd lost everything.

You have helped me to cross a bridge which I could never have crossed by myself.

This morning, when I saw you sleeping after making love, I decided that the time has come for me to go back to San Francisco and face up to things as they really are. In fact, by the time you read this, I'll be at the airport waiting to board my flight.

There's one thing I didn't tell you about Richard. The night after he found out that I'd cheated on him he died in a car accident. The autopsy showed that he was drunk.

Now do you understand why I can't go back to him?

If I've been frivolous and not very well mannered these last few days, this is the reason. I was trying to forget.

Now I know that's impossible.

Yours, yesterday.

Mizuki

PS. I hope you like the gift I've enclosed with this letter. It took me quite a while to translate it.

I look up when I walk
So the tears won't fall
Remembering those happy spring days
But tonight I'm all alone.

I look up when I walk
Counting the stars with tearful eyes
Remembering those happy summer days
But tonight I'm all alone.

Happiness lies beyond the clouds.
Happiness lies above the sky.

I look up when I walk
So the tears won't fall
Though my heart is filled with sorrow
For tonight I'm all alone.
Remembering those happy autumn days
But tonight I'm all alone.
Sadness hides in the shadow of the stars.
Sadness lurks in the shadow of the moon.

I look up when I walk
So the tears won't fall
Though my heart is filled with sorrow
For tonight I'm all alone.

EPILOGUE

Wabi-sabi

As the plane taxied to a halt at El Prat airport, I did what most of the other passengers were doing: broke the rules. I turned on my smartphone before the plane had stopped and waited until it found the local mobile network.

There was a new WhatsApp message, which was a very pleasant surprise.

> Marc has arrived. Just had his first day at home. Dying to meet his godfather. Love from us both. MERITXELL :-)

Risking a telling-off from one of the hostesses, I answered immediately:

> I know it's after 10, but godfather can't wait to meet godson. But I don't know address. SAMUEL xxxx

Three quarters of an hour later the taxi drew up in front of a building in Torrent de les Flors. I unloaded my suitcase and rang the doorbell. A voice on the intercom said "Samuel?" That confirmed, the door opened with a loud buzz.

I went up the stairs with an unfamiliar feeling of excitement in my heart.

Meritxell, smiling proudly, waited for me at the door. I hugged her and we went inside. I was slightly shocked by the dirty clothes piled on a chair, the dishes in the sink and the window with its crooked broken blind but realized that I wanted to help her tidy up the mess.

"He's just woken up. Come and see..."

I leant over the cradle and stared at the tiny boy, who was just four days old. I'd read somewhere that newborn babies can't see or smile, but I had the impression that he was happy to see me.

I took his little hand and he yawned, slightly moving his head, which was covered with a fine fuzz of dark hair.

"He likes you," said Meritxell. "One of my colleagues was here earlier, and Marc cried every time she touched him."

"Do you really think he likes me?"

"Yes – babies are little Buddhas, and they know lots of things. Marc already knows you'll be important in his life."

I put on a serious face, but really I was trying to hide my emotion.

"I'm the godfather, so I can demand to see him every day if I want. I've accepted my responsibility for his upbringing."

"You can come whenever you want. Do you want to hold him?"

Overcoming my fear that I might inadvertently hurt this little creature, I put one hand under his back, which was no bigger than a book, supported his round head with the other hand and held him close to my chest. He made a guttural sound and settled into my arms.

"You're really good at this. You look as if you've been picking up babies all your life. Do want a glass of wine?"

I accepted without taking my eyes off the baby. As Meritxell opened a bottle of red, I joked: "I don't know who his biological father is, but I can tell you that Marc doesn't look like him. He looks like his godfather."

"If you say so."

She poured me a glass of wine and sat down opposite me. She seemed surprised to see that the baby was so relaxed with someone he'd only just met. I admiringly thought that, four days after becoming a mother, Meritxell hadn't lost a single iota of her effortless beauty.

"Are you serious about coming every day?"

"If you don't mind of course..."

"I'd love you to come." Her eyes were shining. "Marc would too. I only asked for your sake."

"Don't worry about me. The summer's long and I don't have to go back to work till September. My only fear is that I might fall in love with you."

Mertitxell flashed me an impish smile. "If that happened, it would be very strange to start a relationship with someone who has a newborn son when you're not the father."

"Nothing's perfect, as I've recently discovered. I may not have fathered Marc, but it doesn't mean I can't love him as if he were my own son."

She frowned as if she thought I was just fooling around. She took my glass of wine, had a sip and then said, "I don't know what you've been up to in Japan, but you're like a new man."

"I hope I haven't changed for the worse."

"On the contrary – you're not so uptight. I knew it! You really needed to do that trip."

"Maybe, but what I learnt there I could just have easily learnt here."

"What did you learn?"

"That only idiots go a long way to try to find what is nearby. That things never turn out the way you want them to. That nothing is perfect and nothing lasts for ever. That everything changes… like Marc. While I'm holding him, we can't see it, but he's growing and already discovering the world."

Meritxell leant forward to stroke my cheek and then asked: "If everything is changing… then where are we now?"

"In a place where everything is possible."

Acknowledgements

To Izaskun Arretxe, the publisher who, after so many years, made it possible for me to finish this book, my thanks for all her patience and enthusiasm.

To Marina Penalva, the first person to believe in this novel.

To Katinka Rosés, Àlex Rovira and Albert Valero, for their company on my three trips to Japan.

To Hèctor Garcia who, without having met us, welcomed us like a good friend in Tokyo.

To Helena Pons for checking the Japanese expressions.

To Marisa Tonezzer who, at one point, encouraged me to write Love in Small Letters.

To Sandra Bruna, my agent and guardian angel.

To all my readers.

Thank you for the privilege of sharing this adventure with you.